YOU BELONG WITH ME

A WITH ME IN SEATTLE NOVEL

KRISTEN PROBY

AMPERSAND
PUBLISHING, INC.

You Belong With Me
A With Me In Seattle Novel
By
Kristen Proby

YOU BELONG WITH ME

A With Me In Seattle Novel

Kristen Proby

Copyright © 2020 by Kristen Proby

All Rights Reserved. This book may not be reproduced, scanned, or distributed in any printed or electronic form without permission from the author. Please do not participate in or encourage piracy of copyrighted materials in violation of the author's rights. All characters and storylines are the property of the author and your support and respect are appreciated. The characters and events portrayed in this book are fictitious. Any similarity to real persons, living or dead, is coincidental and not intended by the author.

Cover Design by Jay Aheer

DEDICATION

This book is for Rachel Van Dyken, without whom it may not have come to fruition.
Thank you for your encouragement, and your friendship.
I love you.

SEATTLE

PROLOGUE
~ELENA~

Twelve Years Ago

I've always hated this room. My father's office is grand, full of honey oak bookcases, a massive chandelier, and a desk in the center of the space that's bigger than the bed I sleep on. Floor-to-ceiling windows are at his back and look out over the estate that he insisted on but, in large part, ignores.

Whenever I'm due for a massive lecture, this is where he drags me.

"May I please speak with you?"

"What is it?" He doesn't look up from his computer, which doesn't surprise me. Paying attention to his daughter has never been a priority for this man. I'll just share my news and go straight to my room, pack my things, and be out of here for good.

I can almost *smell* the freedom. I can't wait to

move in with my husband. *My husband.* That word makes me want to spin in circles of excitement. Archer and I will make a home and have babies. His family is wonderful, and there will be so much love in our household. Our kids will never question whether we love them. They'll never be afraid. And when the time comes, they'll be able to marry whomever they please.

"I got married." I square my shoulders and lift my chin. "Three days ago."

I'm not afraid of my father. Not now. But my stomach quivers with butterflies. I'm eighteen years old. An adult. And I'm able to make my own decisions without influence from my parents.

What can he do? What's done is done.

He looks up from his desk, and his cold eyes narrow.

"And who, exactly, did you marry, Elena?"

"Archer Montgomery."

He sets his pen aside and leans back in his big, black chair, silently watching me. His calculating stare makes me want to squirm, but I hold steady.

"Isn't that the boy I told you to stop seeing a year ago?"

"He's a good man, Dad. If you'd just give him a chance—"

He stands and paces behind the desk, looking out the windows and shoving his hands into his pockets.

Maybe he'll just tell me to leave. That would be the best-case scenario.

"What is your last name, Elena?"

"Montgomery."

"Don't." His voice isn't loud, but it's firm.

"Watkins."

He turns and stares at me impassively. "That's right. And that last name, along with the Martinellis', holds more weight than you can ever fully understand. It means that, as my daughter, you don't have the freedom to marry whomever you choose, whenever you decide to do it."

"I'm an adult."

"You're *my daughter!*"

I blink at the spurt of anger. He's not impassive now. His eyes shoot daggers at me, and sweat breaks out across my skin.

"Dad, I love him."

He shakes his head and waves off my comment as if it's an annoying fly buzzing around his head.

"We'll have it annulled immediately."

"No."

He lifts an eyebrow. I've *never* told my father no. I don't think anyone in his life ever has.

No one would dare.

"Excuse me?"

I lift my chin again. "No."

He stalks around his desk and grips my arm just

above my elbow, almost painfully, and drags me through the house, up the stairs, and into my bedroom.

"You're putting me in time out?"

"I should have done this a long time ago. You're too spoiled. Too indulged. You think you can defy me, go against what's best for the family like this?" We keep moving quickly through the room to my closet, where he pulls a sash off my robe, yanks my arms above my head, and ties me to the light fixture in the middle of the room. He steps back, barely breathing hard. "This is where you'll stay until you come to your senses."

And then he walks out.

"Wake up."

I open my eyes and moan in pain. My shoulders are screaming. My hands are numb.

"Uncomfortable?" my father asks.

I don't reply.

"Was sixteen hours enough time for you to reevaluate your decisions?"

"Dad." I lick my lips. My voice isn't whiny. I'm not a little girl begging for a pony. I'm a grown woman, trying to reason with another adult. "What's done is done. We're married. We love each other. I didn't do anything to hurt anyone, and I didn't want to defy you. If you'd just give him a chance, I know you'd like him."

"It's not about *liking* him, daughter." He sits on my bench. He's in his usual uniform of slacks, a dress shirt, and a tie. He wears this every day of his life. "You're betrothed to Alexander Tarenkov. You've known that since you were twelve."

"I've never met that man in my life."

"It doesn't matter."

"This is ridiculous. I'm not marrying a stranger. This is the twenty-first century. Women can marry who they want."

"Not mafia women."

"I didn't choose this."

"It's a privilege," he insists. "You were blessed with this by birthright, whether you like it or not."

"I'm not divorcing Archer. I'm not giving him up, no matter what you say." I'm breathing hard now. The tears want to come, but I will them back. Just the thought of losing Archer sends searing pain through my heart. I can't live without him.

I won't.

"You'll do as you're told."

"No."

"There's that word again." There's an edge to his voice now. One I haven't heard before. "I'm not fond of it."

"Well, get used to it."

"I didn't raise you to be disrespectful to your father."

"You *didn't raise me*. Grandma did. Nannies did. Not you. And certainly not that pitiful excuse for a woman who gave birth to me."

He stands and walks to me. His face is inches from mine, and I can smell the coffee on his breath.

"You will watch your tongue."

"Or what?"

He rears his hand back as if he's going to slap me, but I stare him in the eye and tilt my head.

"You won't hurt me. The mafia doesn't hurt their women, remember?"

But he does. He follows through and slaps me across the face. The coppery taste of blood fills my mouth.

"I'm not just your father," he says calmly as he walks away and sets a briefcase I didn't see earlier on the bench. He snaps it open. "I'm a mob boss. I'm the one who protects the family, who oversees *everything*. Did you think I didn't know about you and Archer?"

My stomach jumps, but I don't reply.

I watch as my father unbuttons the sleeves of his shirt and rolls them up to his elbows. He unfastens the top button of his collar and then loosens his tie before taking it off.

He removes his Rolex and sets it aside, and then

pulls his long, salt-and-pepper hair back at the nape of his neck.

"I know every move you make, daughter." He glances over his shoulder at me. "I gave you some slack to have your little romance. It kept you occupied, and you're right, Archer comes from a good family. You were safe.

"But to have the audacity to run off and get *married* when you knew it would be forbidden? That, I can't forgive. I've been too soft on you. The annulment is already in the works."

"I won't sign it."

He laughs now. "Do you think I need you to sign it? Elena, you disappoint me."

"I'll just marry him again. You can't keep us apart."

He sighs and reaches into the briefcase and pulls out a whip. It's long and well-worn.

"Dad."

He circles the room, walking around me. He rips my T-shirt in two, exposing my back, then returns to dragging the whip, flicking it with his wrist as if he's warming up.

He's just scaring me.

I'm so sick of this shit! Just let me leave so I can be with Archer!

He walks behind me, and to my utter shock and horror, he cracks that whip across my back, sending crazy, searing pain throughout my body.

"That's one," he says, his voice as calm and cool as glass.

I can't believe it. He *hurt* me.

"What's best for the family is always the priority," he says and lashes the whip over my back again, making me cry out in pain this time. "You know this. You *know*."

"I love him," I whisper, and am rewarded with another lash of the whip.

"Do you think I give a fuck?"

More lashes. He counts ten, then pauses and punches my face. I see stars when he hits me square on the nose, and then he picks the whip back up and counts another ten lashes. And when he's done, and I can no longer cry or speak, he simply rolls up the whip and tucks it into his briefcase.

I can't stand anymore. I'm hanging by my useless, dead hands. I can feel the warm blood trickling down my back, soaking my shorts. Blood also runs down my face, and my eyes are swollen.

"It looks like you need more time to think." His voice is calm again. His impassive eyes roam over my face before he turns and walks out, leaving me alone once more.

The lights come on, blinding me.

"The annulment is complete."

My back sings in pain, as does my face. I have a headache the size of Texas. I can't see well.

But I'm going to live through this, and then I'm going to leave. I'm going to run away with Archer. We can live *anywhere*.

"I can get married again."

"Tsk tsk." He sets a laptop on the bench and opens it, then taps some keys. Suddenly, a video of Archer fills the screen. "Looks like he's having lunch with his sister."

Archer and Anastasia.

"This is live," Dad continues as if we're having a conversation about the weather. "Oh, see this man here?"

He points to the corner of the screen where a man I recognize as one of my father's goons sits at a table nearby.

"He's armed and has been given the command to kill them both when they leave this restaurant if you don't make the right decision. Right here, right now."

My eyes fly to his in shock.

"You wouldn't *kill* him." My voice is like sandpaper.

"You underestimate me, little girl. Even after the beating I handed out last night, you still underestimate me. Did you think I'd let you walk out of here and go off with him? Or let you sneak away?"

I can't reply. My eyes are on the man I love as he laughs with Anastasia. Oh, how I wish I was with them.

"I can't believe you're doing this."

"You have two choices. Either he dies, or you do what you were born to do and think of what's best for your family."

Archer is my family!

"Either way," he continues, "you won't be with him. You just need to decide if he lives or dies."

"This is so fucked-up."

"Quite," he agrees. And when I look into his eyes, I can see that he's enjoying himself.

He *wants* to hurt me.

He's getting off on it.

And I don't doubt that he'd kill Archer just to fuck with my head.

"Fine." I lick my bloody lip and feel everything inside myself break. I feel my heart die. How will I go on without Archer? How will I live for the rest of my life without him in it? But Archer losing his life isn't an option. I *have* to keep him safe. "You win."

"There." Father closes the laptop with a satisfied snap. "That wasn't so hard, was it?"

I expect him to untie me, but he turns away and picks up a lighter and lets the flame lick the big ring he wears with a prominent *W* on it. He doesn't wear a wedding band, but he's worn that stupid, gaudy ring every day of his life.

I want to shove it down his throat and let him choke on it.

"And this is so you always remember who it is that you belong to."

Before I can do anything, he presses the hot metal to my skin, high on my thigh, and I scream in pain as he brands me.

He fucking branded me!

I want to claw out his eyes. I want to spit in his face. But I go limp as a rag and wait as he unties my hands and helps me fall to a heap on the floor.

"I'll send a nurse up to tend to those wounds," he says. "And, Elena, if I find out that you have any words with Archer aside from breaking it off, or if you try to see him, I *will* kill him."

I watch his feet as he walks out of my closet, and then I curl in on myself, crying harder than I ever have in my life. Not from the open wounds on my back, or the burning flesh on my thigh.

No, the pain of losing Archer forever is far worse than any physical pain could ever be.

"Hey."

I'm holding the phone close to my ear, eager to soak in every word we say, even though they're going to be painful. He's going to hate me before this call is over.

"Where the hell are you, E? I haven't heard from you in *days*. A man shouldn't go that long without talking to his wife, you know?"

I close my eyes. *Wife.* Oh, how I long to be his spouse. To truly be his until the end of time.

"Yeah, we need to talk about that, Archer. We were really impulsive."

"Planned it for three months," he reminds me. "I don't think that's impulsive."

"Well, it was for me. You know, I think I just got really caught up in the idea of getting married and everything, but now that I've had time to think it over, I don't think this is what I want at all."

He's quiet for a moment. I want to scream, *I'M LYING! HE'S MAKING ME DO THIS TO US!*

But I can't.

"What are you saying, E? Do you want to go back to dating?"

"No." I swallow hard and hate myself for what I'm about to say. "No, I think it's best if we just go ahead and part ways now. Clean break. I'm sorry if I hurt you, Archer, but it's really what I want."

"I can't believe this."

I have to push my hand against my sore mouth so I don't sob out loud.

"You're *breaking up* with me?"

"Yeah. I'm just too young to be tied down, you know? I need to experience life and spend some time alone. You're just not what I want, Archer."

"But we're married." I can hear him pacing on the other end of the line.

"It can be annulled." Even the word tastes bitter in my mouth. It's the last thing I want, but my father was right. Neither of us needs to sign anything for the mob boss of the Watkins family to make it happen.

There's a beat of silence and then he hangs up without saying goodbye. I've just broken his heart, and I hate myself for it.

I hate my family. My father especially.

Rage flows through me, swift and hot. When it burns out, I feel...nothing. I'll never let anyone hurt me like this again.

Seattle

1

-ELENA-

Beep! Beep! Beep!

I roll over and kill the alarm. I've been awake for at least an hour already, lying in my warm, cozy bed, watching the sky turn from black to purple to blue. I've always been an early riser, which is why my job is so perfect for me.

Baby animals need their breakfast, and at the Oregon Coast Wild Animal Rescue, I'm the lucky woman who gets to feed them.

I stretch my arms over my head and then sit up, letting the blankets fall around my hips, exposing my naked body to the crisp morning air.

Summer is waning, and it won't be long before I have to turn on the heat. But I've been clinging to the season with all of my might. Once winter arrives, we'll have more rain and grey days than I care to think about. So, I plan to hold on to these nice summer moments for as long as I can.

I throw a robe around my shoulders, slide my feet into slippers, and pad downstairs to my small kitchen.

I live in what I lovingly refer to as a cottage. That's probably too grand a word for my little cabin in Oregon. My bedroom is a loft upstairs, and down below, I only have a kitchen, a small living space, and an efficient bathroom.

But it's only me here, so it fits me just fine. In the six years that I've lived in Bandon, Oregon, I've never needed more than this.

I come from mansions and a life of privilege, yet nothing has ever made me feel as safe as this.

I pop a pod in my Keurig, set my *Blow me, I'm hot* mug on the counter, and as my first cup of coffee brews, I step out onto the deck that gives me just a tiny peek at the ocean. The sky is clear today, and the wind is calmer than usual, so I make a mental note and promise myself I'll take a walk on the beach this afternoon after work and lunch with my friend, Lindsey.

With another deep breath, I turn back inside and pour some cream into my coffee, then carry it with me into the living room.

This is my typical morning routine, seven days a week, whether rain or shine. I sit on a small pillow in the corner of the room, crisscross applesauce, close my eyes, and begin my meditation.

I go to my happy place in my mind.

It's on a boat at a marina in Seattle with Archer. Even after all these years, following drama and hurt and more shit than I care to dwell on, it's always Archer I think about when I go to my happy place.

His smile. His gentle hands. Archer was my safe place, my constant source of stability in a life that was anything *but* stable.

When you're the daughter of a mob boss, life is damn scary.

Three minutes later, with a clear mind and relaxed shoulders, I retrieve my coffee and go about the rest of my routine. Shower. Makeup. Hair up in a ponytail.

When I'm dressed and have another cup of coffee in my trusty *Girls rule!* to-go mug, I set off for work in my old, rusted-out Buick. Saying it's second-hand is too kind. It was most likely fifth-hand.

But it does the job and gets me to and from just fine.

It also doesn't draw any unwanted attention.

It's a ten-minute drive to the rescue. I park in my usual spot and walk into the nursery, which is dimly lit as soft music plays through Bluetooth speakers.

It feels like a spa. Like someone's going to hand me a robe and a cup of tea and lead me back to a massage room.

But instead, we have mountain lion cubs, raccoon kits, and a baby sloth, all waiting for my attention.

"Hey, Ally."

I smile, used to being called Ally now. I changed my name when I moved to Bandon, complete with a credit history, passport, and driver's license. All after I spent two years in California under a different name. Unfortunately, I ran into a school friend unexpectedly at the vineyard that I worked at and had to run again.

The mob has connections for a girl who needs to disappear.

"Good morning, Chad." I smile at the man, who's feeding one of the mountain lion cubs with a bottle. "How did it go last night?"

"Pretty normal," he says. "Cleaned up a bunch of poop and fed roughly four hundred bottles."

I laugh at the exaggeration, although there have been times when it felt like that many.

"Is everyone healthy?"

"Raccoon kit red didn't want to eat," he says with a frown, nodding at the pen behind me. "Keep an eye on her."

"Will do. Thanks."

We tie strings of different colors around the animals' necks so we can tell them apart from each other and keep accurate records on each one.

I love this job. It's exactly what I always wanted to do, even when I was a little girl. I'm fiercely protective of it, and I don't even care that I work six hours a day, seven days a week since we lost an employee last year and haven't replaced her.

This is where I'm needed, and I love it.

Really. I do.

"Thanks for meeting me for lunch," my friend, Lindsey, says with a happy sigh as we sit in our booth at the diner downtown. "I feel like I haven't seen you in *forever*."

"I know. We had two bear cubs come in a couple of weeks ago after their mother was poached, and they require around-the-clock care. Work's just been really busy."

"Ally, you need to have more than wild animals in your life."

"No." I sip my Coke. "I don't."

"Sure, you do. You're a young, vibrant, beautiful woman. You need a man."

I shake my head.

"A woman?"

I laugh and sip my drink again. "I don't have time or the need for a relationship."

"We make time for the things that are important to us," she says with absolute sincerity in her voice. "I know some single guys—"

"Seriously. I'm fine."

"Okay." She sighs and smiles at the waitress who's just appeared to take our order. "Hey, Kate. I'll have the chicken salad sandwich with fries."

"Taco salad for me," I say, and we pass her our menus. "What have *you* been up to?"

"Work, mostly."

I raise a brow. "Hi there, pot, I'm kettle."

She snorts. "I know, I sound like a hypocrite. The spa has been super busy this summer with the crazy tourist season."

Lindsey manages the spa for a big resort that sits right on the water. I met her three summers ago when I went in for a massage that had been a gift from my boss.

"So, you must have broken things off with Peter?"

She wrinkles her nose. "Peter was a jerk. He brought me coffee to work one day—"

"Totally a jerk."

"—and he also had two donuts with him. He ate them *both* in front of me. I mean, what kind of monster does that?"

"I might have decked him."

"I thought about it." Lindsey shakes her head. "So, yeah, I broke that off. You know what we need?"

"I think you're about to tell me."

"A girls' night out." She smiles, clearly proud of herself, and I shake my head. "Come on, Al, we're not nuns. We should go out and let loose a little bit. Maybe meet a hot dude and have a little fun."

"I work super early in the morning. You remember that, right?"

"Everyone needs a day off. Even you."

"Until we find someone to replace Stephanie, it's not going to happen anytime soon."

Lindsey scowls and glances up at a TV that's silently playing the news above my head.

"Oh, man."

"What?"

She gestures to the TV with her chin. "I used to be obsessed with that family when I was younger."

"What family?"

I turn to look at the TV and freeze.

Matriarch of most powerful mafia family on the west coast dead.

That would be my grandmother.

My grandma is gone.

I watch the words scroll on the screen as blood rushes through my ears, blocking everything out. My grandmother, the most important person in my life, is gone, and I can't talk to anyone about it. I can't call my cousins or my uncle, Carlo, to ask how it happened or to find out when her service is so I can go home for it.

I can't do anything.

"Ally."

I turn and blink at Lindsey, who's now scowling at me.

"Yeah?"

"I called your name like ten times. Where did you go?"

I shake my head. "Sorry, I was just reading about the story."

"The Watkins and Martinelli families always fascinated me," she continues, sprinkling salt on her fries. "I mean, the sons on the Martinelli side? Have you *seen* them? Talk about hot. I might be willing to be a mobster wife if I could snag me one of those."

I blink at the plate of food in front of me. When did it arrive?

"I mean, how weird would it be to be part of that family?" she continues. "I always thought the mafia was something from the 1920s, not modern-day."

I nod, my mind racing.

"You know what? I forgot about an appointment I have this afternoon." I set my napkin on the table and reach for my purse. "I'm so sorry, but I have to go."

"You haven't eaten."

"I'm not really hungry."

"You can have it boxed up."

I shake my head. "That's okay. I'm sorry. Here's a twenty."

I toss the bill on the table and hurry away, trying to control the tears until I'm in my car alone. Jesus, Mary, and Joseph. I'm such an idiot. Acting this way will only draw attention to myself, and it'll have Lindsey asking questions later.

Like...why would the death of an old woman I don't even know make me so crazy?

I hurry to my car. Once inside, I drive away, leaving Bandon behind. Twenty miles later, I enter a Walmart and hurry back to the electronics section.

I can't call my family. They don't know where I am. My grandmother made sure of that eight years ago. I endured four more years of being under my father's thumb before he was sent to prison and was killed there. My mother was also murdered, and my grandmother sent me away, afraid that I would be the next target.

No one knows where I am.

But there's one person I *can* contact. I need to speak to *someone* from my life in Seattle.

I purchase the burner phone, and when I'm safely in my car again, I turn it on and punch in the number I memorized years ago.

I always send Anastasia the same text. Always. But not this time. Because I'm not just checking in to see how Archer's doing.

Me: *Have you seen the news?*

I sit and breathe, close my eyes, and do my best not to dissolve into hysterics. It won't do me any good to sob uncontrollably in the parking lot of a Walmart.

Get it together, Elena.

Less than a minute later, I get a reply.

Unknown: *I did. I'm so sorry, E. How can I help?*

The tears come anyway.

There's nothing Anastasia can do. There's nothing *anyone* can do. I'm on my own. I've been on my own for almost a decade, but I always knew that if push came to shove, I could contact my grandmother, and she'd help me.

But now, she's gone.

I haven't seen or spoken to her in eight years. She warned me then, sternly, that I had to stay hidden, couldn't blow my cover. She said when the time was right, she'd bring me home.

Even when everything went to shit six years ago at the vineyard, she never contacted me directly. My *situation* was handled quickly and quietly without a word from her.

Because one doesn't simply *leave* the mob. Especially the daughter of the boss. There's no way out. But I've had a reprieve. And I pray that I can stay hidden, that she took our secret with her to the grave. I hope that I'm as safe here in my little haven as I was the day I arrived.

I wipe the tears away and reply to Anastasia.

Me: *Nothing to do. I just needed something from home. Been to any new restaurants lately?*

That last line is my usual one, the one that secretly

asks if Archer's okay. The man never stops eating. The response is always the same unless something is wrong.

So far, nothing's ever been wrong.

I need to check on him. To make sure he's safe and that my family hasn't done anything to him, especially after the way my father threatened to kill him.

Unknown: *Nothing new lately!*

That's the right answer.

I wipe the history on the phone, then place it under the tire of my car and drive over it, making sure it's good and smashed before I drive back to Bandon.

I don't even own a cell phone as Ally. I have a house phone at my cottage with old-fashioned voicemail where the few people who call me can reach me.

That's usually just my work and Lindsey. I stick to myself. I don't trust anyone, and truth be told, I'm not good with people. Because letting people get too close means establishing a relationship, and relationships only lead to heartache.

Been there, done that, have the scars to show for it.

I wipe my cheeks all the way home, letting myself cry and feel the absolutely stabbing pain the loss of my grandmother has brought.

I park in front of the cottage, hurry inside, and lock the door behind me. I run up to my bedroom and open the bottom drawer of my dresser.

Under my socks and underwear is a framed photo.

The only one I allowed myself to bring with me when I fled Seattle all those years ago.

In it, I'm about ten, dressed in a white dress. It was my first communion. The mafia may be full of murdering philanderers, but they're staunchly Catholic.

Sitting next to me, smiling down at me, is my grandmother.

I hug the photo to my chest and give in to not only the tears from earlier, but also the sobs that have wanted to come since I saw the news report in the diner.

I wish, with all my heart, that I could go to the funeral. To be there to say goodbye to the best person I've ever known. I owe her that, especially after everything she did for me. But how? I can't be seen. It would blow my cover, and the last thing I need is for the family to find me.

All I know is, as I sit here sobbing, I *need* to go to Seattle. I quickly search my grandmother's name on my iPad and see that her funeral is in two days. I have *two days* to figure this out.

And that just makes me cry harder.

I'm not sure how long I sit there, rocking back and forth, hugging the image of us together, but finally the tears ebb, and I reach for a tissue to blow my nose and wipe the mess from my cheeks.

I carry the photo downstairs with me and pour myself a glass of wine, then curl up on the couch. I didn't take that walk on the beach. I could still go. There are at least two more hours of sunlight left. The beach helps to ground me, clears my head. And God knows I could use a clear head to figure this out. To remind myself that Grandma would *not* want me to go to Seattle for her funeral. Yes, a walk on the beach is exactly what I need.

But I'm drained. I'm so damn sad. I feel helpless.

Just as I resolve to spend the evening right here on the sofa with a bottle of wine and sappy movies on the TV, there's a knock on the door.

I frown. No one ever comes to my door unless they're lost.

Fuck. Did the family discover where I am? Did they come to find me?

My first instinct is to run.

But that's ridiculous. Grandma wouldn't have told anyone where I am, and she literally *just* died.

It's not the family.

Someone is probably lost.

However, when the knock comes again, I stand and tuck my trusty handgun into my shorts, then with the photo still in my hands, walk over to the door and look through the peephole. I feel my knees almost give out at the sight before me.

My eyes must be playing tricks on me. Maybe there

was something in the wine. How long had it been in my fridge?

"Elena," he says, loud enough for me to hear through the door. "I know you're in there."

I swallow hard. This can't be happening.

"Open this door, Elena."

Elena.

No one has called me that in eight years.

I open the door and stare up at what must be a figment of my imagination.

"Archer?"

SEATTLE

2

~ARCHER~

I've been watching her for days. It sounds creepy as fuck, but once I found her, I just didn't know what to say. I thought I'd rush to her, yank her into my arms, and kiss her until we were both breathless.

But I couldn't approach her. Memories rolled through me as I watched her. The way we laughed, the long, deep conversations. How I couldn't bear to be away from her for more than a couple of hours, and each time I saw her again, it was a balm to my soul.

God, I loved her.

Instead, all I could do was watch her. At some point, she dyed her hair a shade darker than her natural color, but aside from that, she looks the same. Slim body, gorgeous eyes, and just like the last time I laid eyes on her, her bottom lip wobbles, and those interesting orbs fill with tears.

Except this time, it's not because we're standing in front of the justice of the peace, exchanging wedding vows.

"Archer?"

"Hello, Elena. Can I come in?"

She swallows hard and steps back so I can walk inside her tiny house. She's tucked in this little cabin at the end of a dirt road, all alone in a tiny town on the coast.

I have questions, and damn it, I'm going to get some answers.

"Did you see the news?" she asks.

"No, but Anastasia called me." I want to reach for her, wrap my arms around her and soothe her. But she's standing a good six feet away, cradling a picture frame to her chest. Her body language screams: *stay back*. "I'm sorry."

She nods once and turns away to sit on the couch.

There's an open bottle of wine on the coffee table, and a half-empty glass. So, before I sit next to her, I fill the glass and pass it to her.

"Thanks." She takes a sip and watches me silently for a moment. I can admit, after all of these years of being without her, this isn't exactly how I pictured our reunion going. But I'm letting her take the lead here because she has grief written all over her face. "What kind of car are you driving?"

I frown. "Why?"

"Just tell me."

"It's an Audi."

"Newer?"

"Yeah." I frown harder and then repeat, "Why?"

"My car is kind of a piece of crap, but that's on purpose. I mean, it's not so bad that it stands out, but it's also not nice enough to stand out."

She's doing her best to blend. "I understand."

"I just don't trust it enough to get me all the way to Seattle and back."

"You're not going to Seattle."

"Yes." She sets her glass down with a decisive *thud* and hurries past me and up the narrow set of stairs to a loft. "I am."

I follow her, not willing to let her out of my sight. "Elena, you can't go to Seattle. I don't know exactly what's going on here, but—"

"I'll tell you," she interrupts as she pulls a duffle bag out of her tiny closet and starts throwing things into it. "When my parents were killed, my grandmother wanted to get me the hell out of Seattle. We didn't know which family was responsible for Mom's and Dad's deaths, and Gran was sure whomever it was would come for me next. Rather than let that happen, she gave me a new life, out from under my family's thumb.

"She's the only one who knew where I was. She said she'd bring me back when the time was right, but it's never been right. And, frankly, I like it here. By the way, don't call me Elena. Call me Ally."

"No."

She scowls at me. "Yes. I'm Ally here and have been for six years. I've made a life for myself, and I *like* it. A lot."

"So you're not planning to go back to Seattle for good?"

"Hell, no. You know who my family is. I'm not going back to that. But Grandma was the most important person in my life, even if I haven't seen her in eight years." Her chin wobbles again, but she sniffs and pulls herself together. "So, I'm going to her funeral."

"If the family sees you, they won't let you leave again."

"They won't see me."

"Elena—"

"Ally."

"This is crazy. I'm not taking you back there, knowing that your life could be in danger."

To my utter shock, Elena pulls a small handgun on me and levels me with a cold look.

"Yes, you are."

I smirk at the gun. She won't kill me.

"You're right," she says as if she can read my mind. "I'm not going to kill you. But I could take out your knee, your shoulder. Your balls."

I drop the smile and narrow my eyes at her. She's not kidding.

I'm being held at gunpoint by the love of my life.

And she *is* the love of my life. Standing here, looking at her, has me aching. God, I missed her. And I'm smart enough to know that there's so much about her I don't know anymore. She's not the same woman she was when she was eighteen.

But I'm going to relearn her. Because letting her out of my sight again is simply not an option.

"Let's talk about this."

She doesn't blink as she cocks the gun.

I move fast and grip the wrist of her shooting hand as I pull her against me, the gun now pointed away from us.

"I'll take you," I say at last, my nose inches from hers. "But we do it *my* way, and you won't ever pull this shit on me again. After everything you put me through, I deserve better than a gun barrel pointed at my face."

I let her go and walk away, then turn back, soaking her in. "And we're going to talk on the way up there."

She lowers the gun and shoves it back into her waistband. "It's a long drive. I figured we'd talk. I have to call my job."

She pushes her fingers through her long, dark hair and hurries to the side of the bed to pick up a cordless phone straight from the nineties.

She dials a number and waits for someone to answer.

"Hey, Chad, it's Ally. Is Margie in? I was hoping to catch her. She's not? Okay. Well, I've had a family emergency. I need to leave for a couple of days." Her eyes well up again, and it tears at my heart. "Yeah, a death. I know we're already shorthanded, and I hate to do this to you. I know. Family first."

She lowers the phone from her mouth and wipes at a tear.

"Thank you, Chad. Really. I'll call you if I'll be out more than two or three days. Okay. Bye."

She hangs up, and I can't stand it anymore. I cross to her and gently pull her to me.

Elena's arms immediately encircle my middle, and she buries her gorgeous face in my chest, allowing herself a good cry.

I rock us back and forth, rubbing circles over her back and crooning to her.

"It's going to be okay, sweetheart."

She's got a death-grip on my shirt, and her tears rip at my heart. She's clearly hurting, and the only way to help her feel better is to drive her to Seattle.

So it looks like that's what we'll do.

"I wish we'd left last night," she says from the passenger seat, staring out at the pretty Oregon scenery.

"We both needed the sleep," I remind her. She slept hard. I offered to take the couch, but she said that was silly and offered half of the bed.

I took it.

I only touched her once when she whimpered in her sleep, and I reached over to rub her back.

Now that I've found her, there's plenty of time for the rest of it. I don't even know how she feels about seeing me again. But she didn't turn me away, and I'll take that as a win.

"The funeral is tomorrow at two in the afternoon," she says. "At least, that's what the news said."

"I can do a search to confirm it," I reply. "But you can't go in there like this."

"Of course, not. I'll buy a wig and wear sunglasses."

I glance at her and scowl. "You might as well wear a neon sign that says, *This is Elena, hiding from all of you.*"

"Well, what do you suggest I do?"

"I've got this." I reach for my phone and dial my baby sister's number.

"I haven't talked to you in weeks," Amelia says rather than hello. "Where are you?"

"In my car. Hey, I have a special project for you."

Elena grips my arm, and her eyes look panicked. She hisses, "No! Don't drag your family into this!"

"Trust me," I whisper.

"Who are you whispering to? What's going on, Archer?" Lia demands.

"I have someone with me who needs a disguise."

"Between you and Levi, I should go into the camouflage business. What do you need?"

"She can't look *anything* like herself. She's going to a place where if she's recognized, it could mean her life."

Lia's quiet for a moment. "Archer, did you find *Elena*?"

I smile. "Yeah."

"Oh, my God. This is so exciting. Is she with you? Can she hear me?"

"I can hear you," Elena says softly.

"Elena! We've missed you so much. Don't you worry, I'll make you look so different, even Archer won't recognize you."

"I'll always recognize her," I say and link my hand with Elena's, holding on even when she tries to pull away.

She won't be pulling away from me again.

"You can't tell anyone," Elena says, her voice laced with urgency. "This has to be absolutely secret, Lia. Please."

"I understand. Mum's the word. When do you

need me? I have to get some supplies. Are you still the same size?"

Elena and Lia discuss the specifics, and once I've hung up with my sister, Elena bites her lip, looking unsure.

"Talk to me."

"This is a bad idea," she says at last. "What am I doing? I've been safe in Bandon for years. And now you and your family know where I am, and I'm walking right into the lion's den tomorrow. My grandmother would be so pissed."

"You love her," I remind her. "And you're allowed to go to your own grandmother's funeral. You're allowed to grieve and be a human being, Elena. Besides, *I* know where you are, but my family doesn't. And Amelia isn't a snitch."

"I know better than this."

"What are you afraid of?"

She laughs, but it's humorless. "Well, worst-case scenario? You and I are both killed."

"That feels extreme."

"You don't get it. I'm the daughter of a mob boss, Archer."

"A dead mob boss." I glance at her and see her bite her lip again. "And I never got it because you always refused to explain it to me, E."

"Doesn't matter that he's dead." She shakes her head. "I have responsibilities that I walked away from.

There will be punishment for that. Grandmother warned me."

"Your father is *dead*. Who the hell would punish you?"

"Murdered," she agrees. "But it doesn't change the fact that I walked away from the family. That's not okay. I knew I'd have to go back one day, I'm just not ready. And any one of them could punish me for leaving."

I take a deep breath and decide that now's as good a time as any to ask some hard questions.

"Anastasia told me the real reason why you broke things off."

And learning that it was because her father had threatened my life was enough to almost destroy me.

"I wish she hadn't done that."

"So you'd rather I never knew the truth? That I remain clueless? I felt like a fucking fool, E."

"I'd rather you be *safe*," she stresses. "Your safety was always the goal. My father didn't hand out idle threats, Archer. There was no way in hell I was going to allow him to harm you. So, I did what he asked."

"And you never came to find me when he died."

"You don't get it." She growls in frustration. "My father made it clear to *everyone* that if you came around again, looking for me, that you were to be *taken care of*. That directive didn't die with him."

"You didn't give me a chance to make a decision for myself."

"What would you have done?"

"Gone to him," I reply. "Talked to him, man-to-man. Explained that I loved you and that I'd do anything to be your husband."

"It wouldn't have mattered. You're not from the right bloodline. You're not who he picked out for me. And *if* he'd been willing to give you a chance, he would have made you become part of the family. The mob family. And that's not okay, Archer. It would have only made things worse."

"I lost you," I say, frustration flowing through my veins. "It didn't get much worse than that."

"Losing you and the pain that came with it was *nothing* compared to the agony I knew I'd feel if he killed you, Archer. So, yes, I made a decision for both of us, and I'd do it again in a heartbeat."

"No. You won't. You won't ever make a decision like that for me, for both of us, ever again."

"This is ridiculous. I don't know why you're here. Why didn't you just move on? Find someone else and get married. Have a dozen kids. Live your life? Because you being with me puts us both at risk."

"I tried," I admit. "I dated, and there was even someone who loved me enough that I considered marrying her. But it wouldn't have been fair to her because I never would have loved her the way I loved you."

We cross over the Oregon/Washington border, and I feel Elena stiffen beside me.

"No one's going to hurt you, E."

She simply shakes her head once. "They hurt me. Every day. You have no idea."

It's six in the morning when I pull up to my sister's home with Elena. We spent the night in a hotel south of Seattle. Elena didn't trust me to take her to my place, in case it was being watched, and I was inclined to agree.

"You're here," Lia says when she opens the door. She immediately pulls us inside, shuts and locks the door, and then tugs Elena into her arms for a long hug. "Oh, I missed you so much. We have to do all of our crying now so we don't mess up your makeup later."

"I missed you, too," Elena whispers into Lia's shoulder.

After a long embrace, Lia steps back and smiles at Elena. "I always loved your eyes. The one brown and one green is *so* cool, but they'll give you away in a heartbeat."

Now, she's all-business.

"I can't change my eye color," Elena says as we

follow Lia through her home to her studio. "What is all of this?"

"Oh, Archer didn't brag about his baby sister? Tsk tsk." Lia shakes her head at me and smiles at Elena. "I do YouTube videos."

"This looks like more than the occasional video."

"She's being humble," I say. "She has five million followers on YouTube and just launched her own makeup line."

Elena's eyes are huge as she stares at my sister in surprise. The last time she saw Lia, my baby sister was still in high school.

"Wow. Good for you."

"Thanks. Makeup is my jam, and we're going to make you look not only incredible but also completely unrecognizable."

"But how?"

"You're going to look like a man."

Elena and I both blink at my sister.

"There's no way you can make her look like a dude," I say.

"Of course, I can. I have wigs, facial hair, contact lenses to cover those amazing eyes, and I even bought her clothes. She'll be short, but she'll look like a guy in the next six hours."

"Wow," Elena says again. "Let's do it."

For the first time since Elena opened her door to

me yesterday, she has hope in her eyes. If anyone can pull it off, it's my sister.

"I'll be back later to take you."

"Where are you going?" Elena asks.

"I need to get a suit from my house, and I have a couple of errands to run."

"You're not going with me to the funeral."

I shove my hands into my pockets, ready to go to battle. "Yes, I am. I told you we were doing this my way, and there's no way I'm letting you go in there without me."

"Then what's the point of this disguise? If you're with me, it'll be a red flag. You *can't* be there."

"You're not going in there alone." I pace away, frustrated all over again because she's right. If someone from her family sees me there, they'll know she's close by. I look at my sister and then Elena. "I don't want you going in there alone. So, Lia goes with you."

"Great idea," Lia says. "I'll put on a disguise of my own, and we'll look like a couple. We're about the same height. If I wear flats, we'll totally pull it off."

I nod, but Elena shakes her head no.

"I can't let you do that, Lia. It's too dangerous."

"She goes with you, or you don't go at all." I cross my arms over my chest, not willing to budge on this.

Lia nods in agreement. "No one will recognize us."

"I don't like it," Elena says, but then sighs in defeat when she sees the hard look on my face. "Okay."

"You don't have to like it. Keeping you safe is the most important thing." I cup her cheek, wanting nothing more than to kiss her, but we're not there yet. "I'll be down the street from the church in my car. I won't be far."

"Is he always this bossy?" Elena asks Lia.

"Yeah. He's the alpha type."

"I'm right here." I stare at them both, but they just smile back. "I can hear you."

"We'd better get to work if we're going to be ready to go on time," Lia says, gesturing for Elena to take a seat. "Would you rather have dark or light hair?"

"Let's go blond," Elena says. "And maybe spiky. Can you give me tattoos?"

"Like, on your neck?"

Elena nods.

"Heck, yes. Should it be a girl's name? That's super classy."

They giggle as they get down to business, acting as if they've been friends forever and saw each other just last week.

Elena always fit in well with my family. They accepted her unconditionally, and Elena spent a lot of time at our house while we were dating.

I, however, did not get the same reception from Elena's family. In fact, I never met them. Even when we ran away to get married, I never met her parents. Elena told me about them and explained that it wouldn't be safe if they found out about us.

I guess I just blew it off because I was in love, and I was young enough to think that love would conquer anything.

Until one day, she ghosted me. She was my wife, and she just disappeared, then called and said I wasn't what she wanted. I was fucking devastated. Angry. Hurt. It took years for me to move on.

"What do you think?" Lia asks, pulling me out of my thoughts.

After only ten minutes, Elena's face has already changed. I barely recognize her.

"You're a damn genius."

My sister grins and turns back to Elena. "I know. But thanks for acknowledging it."

Seattle

3
~ELENA~

"Oh, God, why did I think I could do this?" I whisper as I drive Amelia and me into downtown Seattle where the funeral is being held. The thing about my family is, despite being kind of scary, they're also quite famous in the Pacific Northwest, so they needed a big church to accommodate all of the people that would come to pay their respects. Which works well for me, as it'll be easier for Lia and me to go unnoticed.

"No one is going to recognize you," Lia assures me and shifts in the seat next to me. Frankly, I don't recognize either of us.

I'm in a man's suit, black with a silver tie. My hair is blond and *not* spiky like I originally thought. We decided to go more conservative than rebellious. But I have a full beard, both of my eyes are brown, and I have sunglasses tucked into my pocket, just in case.

Lia covered her long, blond hair with a brunette wig. We both have prosthetic noses on, giving our faces an entirely different shape.

I park a block down from St. James Cathedral in downtown Seattle. I'm not willing to admit it, but I feel better knowing that Archer's parked not far from here.

I've been to this particular cathedral many times in my life, usually for baptisms and weddings. My parents' funerals were held here, but I didn't go.

I was already far away by then.

We're not early. I wanted to be right on time, when the church would already be full. My family never starts anything on schedule because they like being the center of attention, and they want to make sure the venue is packed.

Judging by the size of the crowd still outside of the church as we drove past, I'd say that hasn't changed in the past eight years.

"We're just going to slip into the back pew," I say for the fifth time since we left Lia's house. "If there's an open casket, which I would suspect there will be, we'll join the line to view her, but only if we can get in the middle of a line."

"You don't have to go," Lia reminds me before we exit the car.

"Yeah, I do. She was the most important person in my life, Lia. I need to say goodbye to her."

Lia nods and reaches over to pat my hand with hers. "Let's do this, then."

We get out of the car and link hands as we walk down the sidewalk to the cathedral. I'm relieved to see that I was right.

The crowd out front is big. People slowly filter into the church, mingling and chatting as they do.

"I guess one thing that never changes over the years is that funerals are social occasions," I mutter.

And now it's time to put on the show of my life.

I act the part of a man, escorting the woman he loves. My hand is on the small of Lia's back as I lead her up the steps and inside the church. So far, I haven't seen any of my family, which is a feat in itself since there are so many of us.

The church is massive inside. Hushed. Stained glass and old architecture surround us. The building is an architectural masterpiece, and I've always loved to look at the stories in the glass.

My goal is not to speak to anyone. I may look like a guy, but there's no way to change my voice, so Lia's agreed to do all of the talking.

It seems the family isn't here yet, which doesn't surprise me. Even though they do all kinds of shady crap, they like to be on display. So, it makes sense that they'd wait for the rest of the onlookers to be seated before they enter the sanctuary.

Grandma's casket is at the front of the church, and it's open.

"Let's go look before the family arrives," I whisper to Lia. She nods, and with our hands linked, we join the line of mourners waiting their turn to see my grandmother.

The closer we get, the bigger the ball in my stomach becomes. It's real. She's really gone.

When we reach the casket and stand near her head, I sigh deeply as I stare down at the woman who loved me so fiercely.

She looks peaceful. They have her in a red dress with her favorite signature strand of pearls. Her hair is salt and pepper and perfectly styled in the way she always wore it.

It looks as if she's sleeping, like she might wake up at any moment, smile at me, and suggest we have crepes for breakfast.

I want to reach in and touch her. I want to kiss her.

But as far as anyone knows, I'm a stranger, and it would only bring attention to myself.

"Let's go," Lia whispers.

She's right. We shouldn't hold up the line for too long.

I turn to walk away, heading down the center aisle to our seats in the back. I freeze.

Walking straight toward me is my uncle Carlo, flanked by Shane and Rocco. Carmine just came in the door behind them and is shaking hands with a man I don't know.

As far as I know, Uncle Carlo took over the role of boss. I loved this man. Aside from Grandma, he was the one I had the most in common with. He doted on me, as I was the only girl in the family for a long time.

But I also know what he's capable of, and he scares me more than a little.

No eye contact.

I glance at the floor and do my best to casually walk past him and my cousins. Lia's holding onto my hand.

Get to the back of the freaking church.

It's like I'm walking in slow motion. They're going to see me. One of them is going to *recognize* me.

But no one even gives me a second glance as they walk past and sit in the front pew.

Lia and I return to our seats, and both of us let out a long breath of relief.

"You did great," she says and loops her arm through mine, then leans her head on my shoulder. "The hardest part is over."

I nod, and we sit and listen for the next hour as the priest prays and gives a sermon. Family members get up to talk, sharing memories and stories.

That's the part that makes me cry the hardest. I wish I could do that, too.

Catholic funerals are long. So long. But it's eventually over, and we're all asked to sit and wait for the family to leave the sanctuary first, carrying my grandmother's casket out to the hearse and then on to the cemetery.

I blink and realize that I'm about to lose a contact. They're not comfortable, but until now, they hadn't given me any problems.

I continue to blink rapidly, and sure enough, the lens falls into my hand. I look up just as my cousin Carmine walks past, carrying the front of the casket on his broad shoulder.

His eyes lock with mine.

They narrow.

But he doesn't stop. He keeps walking past, and before anyone else can see me, I slip my sunglasses on my face.

Once the family is gone, Lia and I stand and slip out a side door, avoiding the front of the church where the family climbs into cars to go directly to the cemetery.

I won't go to the graveside service. It's just for the family, and we would absolutely stick out like sore thumbs there. But I did what I came here to do. I said goodbye.

Lia and I walk quickly, but not too fast, to her car. I drove to give the illusion of us being a couple. Once inside, I breathe a huge sigh of relief.

And the tears come.

"It's the adrenaline," Lia says, rubbing circles on my back. "And the grief. That was intense. Let's get back to my place where you're safe, and I'll make you some tea."

I nod and work on pulling myself together. "Can you please let Archer know we're okay?"

She reaches for her phone and dials his number. He's been waiting a block down the road.

"It's done. We're headed back to my place. Okay, see you soon."

The makeup is gone. I've had a long, hot shower, and I'm back in my regular clothes. I walk out to the pool area of Lia's home, where she and Archer are chatting with a man I haven't met yet.

"You look like you again," Lia says with a smile as she jumps up to give me a hug. "How do you feel?"

"A little raw. Sad. Relieved."

My eyes are on Archer's. He's clearly been worried sick. I can see it in the lines around his eyes. I want to cuddle up in his lap, and I know he would welcome that, but I'm not there yet.

I'm too vulnerable, and Archer and I still have some work to do. Who am I kidding, there's no work to do. I'm going back to Bandon. Alone. There's no reason to snuggle him because nothing has changed.

We can't be together.

"I'd like you to meet my husband, Wyatt," Lia says, gesturing to the handsome man who just stood to offer me his hand.

"It's a pleasure. I've heard a lot about you," he says. He has kind eyes.

"I can't say the same," I say with a smile. "But it's nice to meet you, too."

"I was just telling Wyatt that he would *love* the cathedral we were in today. He's an architect."

"You've never been?" I ask, surprised.

"Not inside," he replies. "But it sounds like Lia will be dragging me there soon. I mean, *taking* me there soon."

I sit on the loveseat next to Archer and watch the blue water shimmer in the pool. It's warm today, despite summer almost being over.

"How are you?" Archer asks.

"Exhausted," I reply honestly. "I don't think anyone recognized me, even after my contact fell out. I was afraid that my cousin may have placed me because, of course, he looked at me after the lens fell out, but he just kept walking."

"There's no *way* anyone knew who you were," Lia says with confidence. "You didn't speak, and your disguise was iron-clad. You're safe."

I nod. "Thank you. So much. I don't think I can ever repay you for today."

"You don't need to repay me," Lia says. "You're my friend, Elena. Even after all this time. And friends help each other."

The tears want to come again. God, how I missed this family. The Montgomerys were always so loving, so welcoming to me. I felt at home with them, and it seems that even after all this time, nothing has changed.

I wish things were different. I'd love to make a life with Archer and his wonderful family.

But that's not meant to be, and I have a life in Oregon to get back to.

"We should go," I say, turning to Archer.

He raises a brow. "Where are we going?"

"Back to where you found me, of course. I have work tomorrow, and I need to get out of Seattle."

Lia's face falls. "Can't you stay for a day or two? You can stay here, with us."

"Thank you so much for the offer, but no. I need to go. And as much as it hurts me to say this, I won't be back, Lia. Not anytime soon, anyway."

"But Anastasia hasn't seen you, and she'll be *so* upset."

My head whips around to Archer. "Does she know I'm here?"

"She knows I found you, but I haven't said anything else." He turns to Lia. "Did you?"

"Well, of course not, because Elena told me not to. But—"

"Good." I sigh in relief. "The fewer people who know I'm here, the better. I really do have to go. It's not safe for me to be here. For any of you either."

"I hate this," Lia says as we stand, and she hugs me once more. She's done that a lot today. I know she was young when everything between Archer and me went down, but we always liked each other very much. "Please stay safe. And come home when you can. I've really missed you."

The guilt is swift and deep. I didn't expect to feel so much of that. "Same here. Take care, okay?"

Archer hasn't said much, and once we're in his car and headed out of town, he's still quiet.

"You don't agree with what I'm doing."

He rubs his fingers over his lips. "No. I don't."

"I've been gone for a long time. Grandma didn't ask the family for permission to help me disappear. For all I know, she never told them that she helped me. I just left one day. So, I don't know if they were looking for me. *I don't know anything* about how it went down for them. But it was made clear to me that there would be repercussions for my leaving. Because this isn't permanent. You don't just *leave* the mob, even if you're born into it and involved through no fault of your own."

"If you don't even know if they're looking for you, why do you have to hide?"

"Because they might be. Or worse, the people responsible for my parents' murders could be looking for me. I don't know what they were involved in that caused their deaths. It could have been as simple as being in the family, and someone was trying to teach us all a lesson."

"Why wouldn't your uncle and the others simply retaliate? Kill them all?"

"Oh, they will. Eventually. It's rarely swift. The mafia has a long memory, Archer. Which is why I can't risk my life in Oregon. I love it there, and if they find me, they'll demand I come back to work for the family."

"Work how?"

I shrug. "In any way they need me."

"Christ."

The farther behind us Seattle gets, the more I relax. I truly am exhausted. I lean my head on the passenger window and close my eyes, enjoying the sunshine on my skin.

"Hey, sweetheart. Time to wake up."

I blink my eyes open and frown when I see that it's dark and we're parked in front of my cottage.

"Holy shit, how did I sleep so long?"

"Exhaustion will do that to you," Archer says as I stretch my sore neck. "I tried to wake you when I stopped for gas, but you were out cold."

"I'm sorry that I didn't help with the driving," I murmur but realize he's already left the car and is rounding the hood to open my door.

I'm totally out of it.

"Come on." He holds out his hand for mine and then tugs me out of the car. He has my duffle bag in his other hand and guides me to the door.

Archer has always taken care of me. He's the kind of guy who fills your car with gas and makes sure you're fed. He always used to ask me if I was cold and offer me his sweatshirt.

I still have one of them. And I'm not sorry for never giving it back.

I unlock the door, and we walk inside, turning on the lights as we go.

"Are you headed back to Seattle tonight?" I ask.

"No."

I frown as he sets my duffle bag down and then turns and walks back outside. Before I can look out the window to see what he's doing, he walks back in with a bag of his own, shuts and locks the door, and turns back to me.

"Do you want me on the couch?"

"You're staying?"

"For as long as you'll let me," he confirms.

I sigh. "We clearly have a lot to talk about."

"Agreed. And it's not going to happen tonight. We're both exhausted, E. Let's get some sleep. We can talk tomorrow."

"I really should go to work in the morning."

Archer checks his watch. "It's already the morning. Just past midnight. You only took one day off, and you told them you'd be gone for a few days. Take one more day to rest up, Elena."

"I hate it when you're right."

He grins.

"So, am I on the couch?"

"It's too small for you," I reply, eyeing his broad shoulders and long, lean body. He grew a couple of additional inches after we broke up. "I don't mind sharing the bed."

He nods, and I lead the way upstairs. Despite a six-hour nap, I feel like I could sleep for another twelve.

"Why am I so tired?"

"You had a pretty wild twenty-four hours," he reminds me. "The adrenaline of not wanting to be recognized, the grief of the funeral. All of it. It's intense, and your body is ready to rest."

"You're not kidding."

"Can I use your shower?"

"You can use whatever you like," I reply as I shuck out of my shoes and stand in the middle of the room.

"I usually sleep naked, but that probably won't work tonight."

"Not if you want me to keep my hands to myself."

I glance at him. "*Not* keeping your hands to yourself will only complicate things. So, I'll find something to sleep in."

"We're as complicated as it gets, honey." He kisses my forehead. "Go to sleep. I'm gonna wash up. I'll be back in a few."

I nod and watch him walk back down the stairs before I turn to my small dresser and forage for an old tank top and a fresh pair of panties.

I *love* having Archer here. And that's a problem. I can't get used to it. I can't just fall into his arms because that's where I feel safe. Because it feels good. I have to be smarter than that. He'll be gone soon, and I'll be left alone all over again.

I can't get used to him.

I hear the water running in the shower as I decide to quickly change the sheets on the bed. Sleeping in fresh bedding is the best. Not that I won't sleep like the dead anyway.

I've just slipped the cases on the pillows and slid between the sheets when Archer walks up the stairs.

"You must be tired," I say, watching in rapt fascination as a mostly naked Archer walks around my little loft-slash-bedroom. He's a big man, making the room feel even smaller than it is. And holy hell in a handbasket, his body has only improved with age.

He was something to write home about when he was twenty. At thirty-two? He's ridiculous.

It's definitely good that I'm wearing clothes. And that I'm so tired.

Okay, maybe I'm not *that* weary.

I shake my head and push my hand through my hair. *Pull it together, Elena.*

I mean, Ally.

I'm Ally.

Archer slips into bed next to me and reaches over to extinguish the light. In the darkness, we lie down, and my eyes instantly close. I've always felt safe here in my little cottage.

And now, with Archer here, as well, I feel protected. It's amazing.

And fleeting.

SEATTLE

4
~CARMINE~

"I'm telling you, she was there," I repeat and lean over my father's desk, staring him in the eyes. "Elena attended Grandmother's funeral."

The thought still cuts me to the core.

"And why didn't you say something *then*?" Pop asks.

"Because I had Grams' casket on my shoulder. It wasn't exactly the time or place."

Rocco paces behind me. My brother shares my frustration. We were close to Elena, raised together like siblings rather than first cousins. In fact, there's nothing that my brothers and I wouldn't do for her.

She *knew* that.

So why did she run? And where the fuck has she been?

"She was disguised as a man," I mumble, turning

to pace the office, as well. "But when she looked up, her eyes gave her away."

"I can't believe she could pull that off," Rocco mutters.

"Where has she been?" I demand, turning back to my father. "Do you know?"

He puffs on his cigar, sits back in his big, black chair, and seems to think it over.

"I thought she was dead," Rocco adds. "She just vanished."

"When Vinnie and Claudia died, the family was in chaos," Pop reminds us.

"Not so much that Elena would miss her own parents' funeral," I reply and walk to the window of my father's office that looks out over the city of Seattle. "We all assumed that she was killed too, and that we'd never find her."

"Jesus," Rocco mutters. "Who would have helped her leave?"

"Her grandmother," Pop says. "She must have helped her hide so she didn't meet the same fate as Elena's parents. My mother-in-law was a shrewd woman with a wide array of contacts."

"We can keep Elena safe *here*," I growl and turn back to the room.

"Of course, we can," Pop says with a nod. "So, we'd better find her."

"We need Shane," Rocco says. "He's the tracker in the family."

"I'll call him," I reply. "In the meantime, we need to step up the search through Grandmother's things."

"She lived in that house for sixty years," Rocco reminds me. "It's ten thousand square feet containing sixty-years-worth of shit. It'll be like finding a needle in a haystack—if there's anything there at all. Grandma knew how to cover her tracks and keep secrets. She wasn't the wife and mother of bosses for nothing."

"If there's anything there, we'll find it," I reply.

"What if Elena doesn't want to be found?" Rocco asks.

"That's not how this works," Pop says, his voice like steel. "And she knows it. There's no leaving the family, and she's had a long enough reprieve. It's time we bring her home."

I nod once. "I'll go through Grandma's house myself."

"One more thing," Pop says before we can walk out of the office. "Aside from Shane, this doesn't leave this room."

"Understood."

Rocco and I leave Pop's office, and I immediately reach for my phone. It's time for Shane to come home, too.

My brother answers on the second ring.

"We need you here, brother. As soon as possible."

"What's going on?" he asks.

"Elena's alive, and we need to track her down."

There's a long silence as Rocco and I ride the elevator to the parking garage. "I'll be there in seventy-two hours."

"Good." I hang up and slip my phone back into my pocket.

"She's going to be punished," Rocco murmurs, and my gut clenches.

"I know."

"How could she put us in this position?"

"We're going to find out."

SEATTLE

5
~ELENA~

I smell coffee. And bacon.

I don't have any bacon.

I sit up and blink, surprised that the sun rose before me. The bed next to me where Archer was all night is empty and cool.

And it seems he's making me breakfast.

I glance at the alarm clock and sigh before rubbing my hands over my face and through my hair.

It's eight-thirty. I don't remember the last time I slept this late, especially after the long nap in the car yesterday. But Archer's Audi was so comfortable, especially with the heated leather seat, and I just couldn't keep my eyes open.

"You're awake."

Archer carries two plates and two cups of coffee into the room. How he's managing to hold it all is thanks to long arms and muscles for days.

At least he's dressed this morning. Because a mostly naked Archer is *way* too tempting to my long-ignored libido.

"I didn't have bacon in the fridge."

"A travesty I fixed first thing." He grins and sets the dishes on the bed, passing me one of the coffees. "I assume you don't take sugar in it since you didn't have any down there."

"Just cream," I confirm and take a sip, eyeing the eggs, hash browns, and bacon on the plate in front of me. "Where did you get all of this?"

"The grocery store in town." He digs in and takes a big bite of his eggs. "You didn't have anything down there. Are you trying to starve yourself?"

"You still have the same appetite, I see."

He grins and chews some bacon. "Don't worry, I bought us some stuff."

"Archer."

I set my coffee down and turn to him, but he reaches over and picks up a slice of my bacon and holds it up to my lips.

"Eat, E."

"Ally." I take a bite and chew, holding his gaze. "My name is *Ally*."

"Ally what?"

I clear my throat. Lick my lips. *Shit.*

"Ally what?" he asks again.

"Look, thanks for the groceries, but I'm sure you

want to get back on the road so you get home at a decent hour—"

He takes my chin in his fingers and makes me look him in the eyes. "Tell me."

"Montgomery," I whisper and close my eyes in embarrassment. "Ally Montgomery."

"Look at me."

"Archer, it doesn't matter what my last name is."

To my utter shock, he simply leans over and covers my lips with his own. Gently, but boldly. My inhale is sharp, but I don't pull away.

I've dreamed of having his lips on mine for *years*.

And here he is. Kissing me as if he does it all the time, like it's no big thing. Like my heart isn't pounding out of control. Like he isn't going to leave me alone any minute.

When he pulls away, his eyes are dilated, and his breaths come a bit faster than before.

"I'm not leaving."

"Archer."

"Just listen," he pleads. "It took me a long damn time to find you."

"No one was supposed to *ever* find me." I stop short and frown at him. "Wait. How did you find me?"

He pulls a piece of paper out of his back pocket and holds it out for me to take. I recognize the lined notebook paper. It's well-worn, the creases deep as if he's opened and closed it a thousand times.

I unfold it and sigh.

"My list."

"I remember that day like it was yesterday," he says, still eating his breakfast. "You told me all the places you'd run away to if you had the chance, and I wrote them down so I could take you to every one of them someday."

"And you kept it. These were just daydreams," I say, but lovingly read over the words.

Maui

Horse ranch in Montana

California vineyards

Tuscany

Bandon, Oregon

Beach in Mexico

I see each item has notes and check marks next to them, clearly written recently.

"You never talk about something flippantly," he says, making my heart skip another beat. "They may have been daydreams, but I know you, and I knew I'd find you in one of these places."

"I notice you didn't try Maui, Mexico, or Tuscany."

"I decided to start more domestically, but if I hadn't found you here, Maui was next on my list."

I've cried so much over the past two days, I wouldn't have thought I had any more tears left in me. But my eyes well as I stare at the list.

"We were on the boat that day," I say. "Drifting

around Lake Washington, and you just let me talk on and on about these places that I'd like to visit. You were always a good listener, Arch. A good friend."

"I'm still a good listener," he says. "And your eggs are getting cold."

I take a bite of eggs with potatoes and fold the paper, then pass it back to him. "You can't stay."

"Why not? If you don't want me, if you've moved on with your life and you truly want *nothing* to do with me, then I'll go. Is that what you want? To never see me again?"

I can't lie to him. Even if it would be best for both of us. I should tell him that I don't want him, and send him far away.

To keep him safe.

He links his fingers with mine, the way he always did when we were so young and so in love we were stupid with it. And I know that I don't have the strength to tell him to go.

"I want you to be safe," I admit. "That's all I've ever wanted."

"I'm a grown man, perfectly capable of taking care of myself."

"Archer." I surprise us both and straddle his lap, framing his face with my hands. "I need you to *hear* me. I know you're able to take care of yourself, but my family is powerful. Ruthless. And if they find us here, they'll kill you. Don't you understand that everything I've done over the past twelve years has been to keep you safe from them?"

"I don't take this lightly. That's not what I'm saying, E. But the risk of being with you is better than the agony of being without you."

I lean my forehead against his. "We don't even know each other anymore."

"We'll learn." His hands, those big, wonderful hands, glide to my ass, over my loose T-shirt, and then he buries his fingers in my hair. "Maybe we won't like each other anymore, and I'll be gone in twenty-four hours."

That makes me smile. "You have started snoring in your old age. That could be a deal-breaker."

His eyes narrow. "I don't snore."

"Uh, yeah. You do."

He moves fast, pinning me to the bed.

"I think my ass is in my eggs," I say, giggling like crazy.

"Take it back."

"It's the truth. I can feel them through my underwear."

"No, the snoring. Take it back."

"Sorry. No can do. I could have sworn there was a freight train in here last night. But look on the bright side. I didn't have to use one of those white noise machines."

He barks out a laugh and buries his face in my neck, biting the sensitive flesh just under my ear.

"Are you still ticklish?"

Shit. I'm so ticklish.

"Archer, no."

But before he can do his worst, there's a knock on my front door, and we both freeze and stare at each other in surprise.

"No one ever comes here," I say as Archer climbs off of me, and I pull on a pair of sweats over my egg-soaked undies. "Stay here."

I hurry down the stairs and look out the window.

Lindsey's car is parked behind Archer's.

Double shit.

I clear my throat and paste a smile on my face as I open the door to my friend.

"Hey," she says. "I brought you some pastries from Marie's. I heard you've been out of work because of a family emergency. Why didn't you call me? I'm so sorry, Ally."

"Oh, thank you." I accept the box of goodies but don't invite her in. "I've been pretty out of it, and it was a complete surprise."

"I guess so. I mean, I was with you just a couple of days ago, and everything seemed okay. Whose car is that?"

She gestures to Archer's car, and I blink rapidly.

"Oh, it's, um, my—"

"It's mine."

I feel Archer walk up behind me, bracing his arm on the doorjamb above me, and I know he's smiling at my friend. Lindsey's eyes dilate at the tall drink of water standing behind me.

And honestly, I can't blame her.

"Archer," he says, holding out his hand for hers.

"Lindsey," she replies, shaking the proffered palm. Her eyes dart to mine with a silent *what the hell?*

"Archer is a friend of the family. He came to help when he heard the news. He'll be leaving soon." I clear my throat again. "Thanks for the treats, Linds. I appreciate it."

I back away, giving the universal signal for *thanks, now go away.*

And to my surprise, it works.

"Okay. Well, call me if you need anything. Nice to meet you, Archer."

"You, too."

We wave, and I shut the door then close my eyes on a sigh.

"Three days ago, I was safely hidden here. Nothing fishy going on to make me stand out or have people asking questions. Now, it feels like it's all slipping out of control." But it'll return to normal as soon as Archer goes back to Seattle. I know he said he's staying, but that's just not possible. I'll enjoy his company today, but then he has to *go.*

"There's nothing fishy about a family friend coming when there's been an emergency."

"Right. A charming, handsome guy like you is definitely the norm at times like these."

His smile would light up Times Square. "You think I'm handsome?"

"Have you *seen* you?"

"I mean, I clean up okay. I've never had any complaints."

"You're a smartass."

"That hasn't changed, sweetheart. Let's eat these donuts."

"What is it about Bandon that you've always liked so much?" he asks me later as we walk the beach. Large rocks stick up out of the sand around us. They remind me of Stonehenge. Sometimes, when I walk here in the very early morning, I expect to see witches and faeries in the mist. It's a magical place.

"The beach here is beautiful," I reply and step over a dead jellyfish. "There aren't quite as many tourists as northern Oregon, so I'm less likely to run into someone I know. That happened before, in California."

"So, you haven't been here the whole time?"

"No, I was Paige Williams and worked at a vineyard down in California for a couple of years. But one day, a girl I used to go to middle school with came through on a tour and recognized me."

I sigh at the memory and then point out into the ocean as a whale sprays water into the air.

Archer nods but doesn't let me quit the story.

"It's ironic that your last name was Williams. My cousin Natalie married Luke Williams."

"I know." I smile up at him when he glances down in surprise. "I've kept track of everyone. And your family is in the spotlight pretty much all the time."

"True. But you didn't know about Lia?"

"I knew." I shrug a shoulder. "I feigned surprise. I just didn't want to seem like a stalker or something."

"You're a stalker."

I wrinkle my nose. "Curious. I like the term *curious* better. Anyway, after Sheila saw me, I went directly to the place I rented and texted the number my grandma gave me. Within an hour, a man showed up at my door with a packet. No words were exchanged, he just gave it to me and left.

"Inside was my new life. Name, bank accounts, birth certificate, passport, driver's license. The works."

"Wow."

"Yeah, Grandma was impressive. I texted her after I arrived in Bandon and told her I was here but was vague. She didn't want to know specifics in case anyone came looking for me. We always knew how to reach each other, though.

"I *love* it here, even more than California. It was fine there, but I realized that I need to be by the water. It energizes and soothes me. But none of this is what we really should be talking about."

"There's something we should talk about?"

"So many things," I mutter. "Let's start with this. I know you said you're staying, but Archer, that isn't possible."

"I don't have to be in Seattle for a bit," he says as if he's being deliberately obtuse. "I guess I should catch you up on what I've been up to. I sold the fishing boat about five years ago. Now, I buy and sell real estate. Mostly commercial properties, but sometimes, I buy residential places here and there."

"You're a landlord?"

"Sort of. Anastasia works in one of my buildings. She used to live there, too. She makes wedding cakes. She was living above her shop, but since she recently got married, she's now living with her new husband out on one of the islands."

"Anastasia got married?" I feel immediate regret that I didn't know that. That whenever I contact her, I just ask about Archer, never about how she's doing. "Good for her."

"She's happy. She married Kane O'Callaghan."

"The artist?"

"That's the one. Anyway, my point is that I am

self-employed. And as such, I think I'll take a look at some property around here. Mostly out of curiosity."

"I don't know what there is for you to look at," I admit with a gusty breath. "You can't *be* here. It's not safe for you. For either of us."

He stops short and waits for me to face him.

"I'm not trying to make things unsafe, E. I worked so hard to find you. I just want to enjoy you for a while. I'm flying by the seat of my pants here. All I know is that I don't want to leave here without getting to know you again."

I shake my head. "It can't happen, Archer. I wish it could. More than you know."

God, I missed him so much. It still hurts.

"You can't stay."

But he doesn't respond. He just looks down the beach and then gestures with a shake of his head.

"How far are we going?"

"Not much farther." I gesture ahead. "See those two rocks there?"

"The ones a half a mile away?"

I laugh and look up at him. "You're an athletic guy. An extra half-mile won't hurt you."

"You were never the sporty type," he says.

"I decided to start exercising more when all of this started," I admit. "I've always been an introvert. That hasn't changed, but I didn't realize that being isolated could be *so* lonely. And one of the things I found that helps is working out. I do yoga and meditation most mornings, and I like to come out here to walk or run in the afternoon if the weather isn't too bad."

"Run, you say?"

"Sure."

"I'll race you, then."

And he takes off jogging. I pause, just to watch his sexy body from behind. Tight ass, broad shoulders, muscular back. I need to soak it all in because in a couple of hours, he'll be gone, and these few stolen moments on the beach are all I'll have to hold close.

Holy hell in a handbasket, he's hot.

I take off, enjoying the push and pull of my muscles as I sprint closer to him and then run past him, reaching the rocks a good twenty yards ahead of him.

We stop and bend at the waist, trying to catch our breath.

"Holy shit," he says as he works to take in air. "You're fucking fast."

"Been doing it a while." *And I wanted to impress you.*

Which is kind of dumb, but there you have it. The appreciation in his bright blue eyes was worth every step.

"These are nice," he says, gesturing to the houses on the bluffs. "Why didn't you go for one? Looks like several are for sale."

"I don't make that kind of money at my job. I

couldn't afford one of these," I say, shaking my head. "And, yes, my grandmother made sure my bank account has a couple million dollars in it, but it would look crazy if I bought one of these places and then collected my salary. I'd stand out, and the whole point is to blend. Besides, I like my little place."

"It's cute," he agrees. "Small."

"It didn't feel small until you were in it." I laugh and take a deep breath, soaking in the salty air. "It's always just been me."

"Always?"

I know what he's asking. Has there been anyone since him?

"I haven't been a nun," I admit, making him scowl. "But I haven't been in a serious relationship since you, Archer. How could I when the entire relationship would be based on lies? I couldn't even tell him, whomever he may be, my real name. You can't build anything on lies. And I have to be ready to leave at a moment's notice. So, yes, it's always just been me in my cottage."

"I shouldn't be jealous," he says. He's caught his breath, and with his hands in his pockets, he stares out at the water. "It's been a long time, and of course, you're not a nun. But I'm jealous all the same. And relieved."

"Relieved that I'm an old maid?"

He turns to me now. "You're not an old maid. But I am relieved that you don't belong to anyone."

"I belong to *me*. And that's how it will always stay, Archer."

He nods once and wraps his arm around my shoulders, pulling me against his side. "What are you going to feed me for dinner?"

"We literally ate lunch right before we came here."

"That was at least an hour ago."

"How do you eat so much and still look like this? It shouldn't be possible."

"Genetics." He kisses my hair, and I melt against him. Archer was always physically affectionate. It was something I had to get used to because my parents were distant, and the only one I was close to who hugged me was Grandma.

I didn't realize I was so starved for touch.

But not just any touch. Archer's.

I fit against him perfectly, my shoulder under his armpit. My arm around his waist. His lips planted on the top of my head.

I don't want it to end.

"We could do spaghetti," he suggests, making me laugh. "You always made a really good sauce."

"It's gotten better since I last saw you."

"Don't tease me," he says. "My fragile stomach can't handle it."

"I'll prove it. And just so you know, I know this trick. I'm not giving in to your reverse psychology."

"You totally are. It's okay. I'm charming, remember?"

"I never should have told you that. It just inflates your ego." I stop and turn into him, burying my face in his hard chest, clinging to him with everything I have. "You can't stay, Archer. This is me digging in my heels and telling you *no*. You can't stay in Bandon."

He doesn't say anything for a long moment, just brushes his fingers up and down my arms, and then circles his arms around me and pulls me close.

"You've been the love of my life since I was a junior in high school and I saw you sitting with Stasia in the cafeteria. You're *everything*, E, even after all this time. And that won't ever change."

"Archer—"

"Listen." He catches my chin with his finger and makes me look him in the eyes. His are that insane bright blue and churning like the ocean behind him. "You're *everything*. It feels like I've loved you my whole life."

He always was good with words.

He doesn't say anything else about staying with me. That was the best goodbye speech I've ever heard. He deserved to hear something that amazing when I left him all those years ago.

But I was young and didn't know what the hell to

do, except get as far away from him as possible. To keep him safe. To keep him *whole*.

We're quiet on the walk back to the cottage. To my surprise, Archer strides right up the stairs to the loft and starts gathering his things, filling his bag.

"You don't have to leave tonight." I'm such an idiot, sending him mixed messages. But the thought of watching him walk away tears at my heart. "You could stay and get a fresh start in the morning. I'll make the spaghetti."

"It's okay." Once his bag is tucked in his car, he walks back up the steps to the front door and leans on the jam, smiling down at me in that way he always used to when he was particularly amused by me.

I have no idea what's so damn funny about this. We're saying goodbye for good.

"Thank you for coming. For taking me to Seattle. For everything."

He pulls me in for another hug, holding me firmly.

God, this is killing me. Why did he have to come here in the first place?

"I love you, Elena," he whispers. He kisses my forehead and then my lips. I feel it all the way to my toes, even though it's the barest brush of skin against mine.

Without another word, he turns and jogs to his car, fires up the engine, and drives away.

"It's the right thing to do," I mumble as I close the door and lean against it, willing the tears to stay back.

It may be the right thing, but it still hurts, all the way to the bone. My cottage feels emptier than it ever has. "Get used to it, *Ally*."

I square my shoulders and get down to business, cleaning and scrubbing my little house and getting ready to return to the safe life I've made for myself in Bandon, Oregon.

To my surprise and delight upon returning to work this morning, I discovered that Margie hired a new employee. Which means I'll start to have days off here and there, and Chad and I won't be so slammed.

I almost kissed Margie on the mouth when she told me, but there was no time.

I immediately shifted into training mode and spent all day showing Beverly the ropes. It was a satisfying but tiring day.

Now that I'm home, I'm ready to go for my usual afternoon walk and then settle in for some alone time.

With my cropped yoga pants and tank top on, I set off for the beach, taking the same route I took with Archer just yesterday.

I hope I was able to cover the anguish I've felt since he left last night. If I looked sad at work today, maybe the others chalked it up to the family emergency that took me away from work, and not to me feeling heartbroken over someone I lost more than a decade ago all over again.

The beach is pretty much abandoned as I walk south. Fewer tourists is another sign that summer is almost over, and we're headed into the winter months. I'll miss the warmer weather and the sunshine.

I'm usually energized after my walks, but when I return home, I just feel tired. So, I take a quick shower, change into my comfies, and place an order for pizza delivery.

I'm going to give myself this one night to wallow in self-pity, and then it's back to business as usual.

When I'm armed with a large pepperoni, a full glass of wine, and the remote, I settle on the couch with my favorite blanket and snap on the TV. The regional news fills the screen.

"From what we've been told, law enforcement believes the Martinelli family may be behind this brutal murder, but the investigation is ongoing."

I quickly turn the channel to the home improvement network and set my pizza aside.

This. This is why I turned Archer away.

And it would be best if I didn't forget that.

SEATTLE

6

~ARCHER~

I could have stayed with her last night, but I have a shit ton to do in a short time. If she thinks I'm leaving, she obviously doesn't know me very well.

But I'll be happy to remind her.

Because I'm not going anywhere. If she needs space and time to get used to the idea of having me around, that's fine with me.

I'm in no hurry.

I've temporarily settled myself in a suite at a seaside resort, and I have a meeting with a real estate agent in fifteen minutes. I've had breakfast, and a five-mile run already, and am on my way to look at the house that caught my eye yesterday when I was on the beach with Elena.

Ally.

I need to get used to her name. She has my last

name. I wonder if that's a coincidence or if she told her grandmother what name she wanted to use. She *should* have my name. And she would if she hadn't been afraid of her father.

"Mr. Montgomery?"

I nod at the woman standing by the front door of the large house on the cliffs. I can hear the waves crashing in the distance. "Yes, ma'am. Ms. Stebbins?"

"Cheryl, please." She shakes my hand and then opens the already unlocked door. Cheryl knows how to do her job well. She's an attractive woman, dressed in a simple, classy suit. Her blond hair is styled in waves down her back, and I can see she recently applied red lipstick to her pouty lips. But her smile isn't flirtatious, and she's all-business when she gestures for me to walk in ahead of her. All of the lights inside are already on. "This particular house has been on the market for about five weeks."

I nod again. I did a little research on this property last night while I ate takeout in my hotel room. The main living space is bright and open, with floor-to-ceiling windows that give me an unobstructed view of the ocean beyond. The furniture looks new, is simple, and fits the space perfectly. "Is it possible to buy the furniture with the house?"

"I'm sure we can make an offer and see what they say. They've already moved out of state."

The views from the kitchen and living room and then the master bedroom are simply stunning.

"The house was built in 1982, but as you can see, the current owners completely remodeled the home, updating all of the rooms."

"It's nice," I reply, taking in the white kitchen with black lower cabinets, the up-to-date light fixtures, and brand-new floors. It's better than nice. It's gorgeous. Living here while I win my girl back won't be a hardship in the least. "I'll take it."

Her eyebrows climb, and those red lips part in surprise. "Just like that?"

"Just like that."

"Do you have preapproval for a loan?"

"I'll pay cash. I'd like to close as soon as possible. And I'd like to ask the owners if I can move in right away, paying them rent, of course, until the closing date."

"Like I said, they've left the state, so I don't think that will be a problem."

"Great. You'll be able to reach me all day should you need to."

"This could be the easiest sale of my career," Cheryl says as we walk outside, and she locks the door behind us. "I'll start making calls and drawing up the paperwork right away. I'll call the current owner and get back to you today regarding your questions."

"Thank you, Cheryl."

I shake her hand again and then lower myself into my car, headed back to the resort. The first matter of business for the day is finished. If E—*Ally* won't let me stay with her, I'll buy my own place. It's a good investment anyway.

I hurry back up to my suite and call my assistant, Leslie.

"Are you coming into the office today?" she asks when she answers the phone.

"No. I'm going to be working remotely for a while, Les."

"Killing me, boss."

I smirk and open my laptop. "There's nothing you can't handle in that office."

"You bet your ass about that," she says. "But I can't sign your name or write million-dollar checks. That's above my pay grade."

"No one writes million-dollar checks," I say as I press my finger to the pad on the keyboard and log into the computer. "We do everything electronically these days. Speaking of, I just bought a property in Oregon."

She's quiet for a moment, and I can just imagine the frown on her pretty face.

"Oregon?"

"Bandon, Oregon, to be exact."

"Commercial property?"

"A house. One that I'm going to be living in for a bit, and then I'll lease it out."

"I'm sorry, am I speaking to Archer Montgomery?"

"I don't pay you extra to be a smartass."

"You should. My smartassery is deeply undervalued. What are you doing in Oregon, Arch?"

"Let's call it a working vacation. I'll have my home office set up soon. You can reach me anytime."

"I have a list of messages for you," she says. "And you haven't answered your email in three days."

"I'll work on that today."

"Are you okay, boss?"

"I'm great. Better than I've been in a long time. But, Les, where I am is confidential. If anyone asks, I'm just out of town."

"That's the answer I give anyway. Please, and I mean this most sincerely, check your email."

"I promise, I'll do it today. I'll keep you posted."

"Be careful."

She hangs up, and I grin. Leslie's been with me since I started the business five years ago. She knows more about the day-to-day than I do, and that's no lie. We joke about her lack of compensation, but I pay her well for the job she does for me.

She's worth every penny.

Feeling confident that Leslie has the home front taken care of, I briefly think about what I should have for lunch, but my phone interrupts my decision making.

If Cheryl's calling already, it's either very good or very bad news.

"Hi, Cheryl."

"I have some excellent news for you, Mr. Montgomery. The sellers have agreed to your terms and are willing to include the furniture with the full price offer."

"Excellent."

"As I mentioned, they've moved out, so all of their personal effects are gone."

"When can I move in?"

"Immediately." She laughs as if she can't believe it. Truth be told, neither can I. "We have some paperwork to take care of, and then it's all yours."

"Excellent."

Four hours later, I've checked out of the resort and am unpacked in my new ocean-front house in Oregon. Setting up my office didn't take long, given that the desk and chair, along with shelves were already in the room. All I had to add was my laptop. I will need to find a store soon for a printer-slash-scanner, and I'm sure Leslie will give me a list of things I'll need, but this will work just fine for now.

I made a grocery run to stock up on the essentials, which for me is roughly five-hundred dollars-worth of food and snacks, some cleaning supplies, and a few bottles of the wine I saw at Ally's house.

Now, despite all of the food in the place, I decide I'm too tired to cook, so I drive to town and walk into the diner. I sit in a deep red booth, looking forward to the burger and fries I just ordered.

"Archer?"

I glance up, and there's Ally's friend from the other day.

"That's your name, right?"

"Yes, and you're Ally's friend…"

"Lindsey."

"Right. Nice to see you."

"You, too. I guess I'm confused. I saw her today, and Ally said that you left yesterday."

"Did she?"

"Yeah. She didn't look great, actually."

My heart stops, and my eyes narrow. "What do you mean?"

"Pale, quiet. I figured she was just still getting over the family emergency she went through. But here you are."

"Here I am."

I don't ask her to join me. That's not appropriate. But I also don't want her to rush off and call Ally. I want the news that I'm still here to come from *me*.

"I had some business to see to, and I didn't want to leave until I knew she was okay. I'll look in on her before I head out of town."

Lindsey's shoulders sag, and a smile spreads over her lips. "I understand. I'm glad she has you as her friend. I wish she'd told me about you before. I always thought Ally was a lonely person, but maybe she's just private."

"She's definitely private," I agree. "Have a good night, Lindsey."

"You, too."

She waves and walks up to the counter where a bag of food is ready for her to take away.

In a town as small as this one, I won't be able to be here for long without Ally knowing it. And that's okay, it's not a secret. But until this minute, I didn't realize how much I wanted her to find out from me, not someone else.

So, I'll have to make sure I *run into her* tomorrow and get going on my plan to win her over.

She never did go for flowers. She wouldn't turn them away, but posies aren't the way to El—Ally's heart.

Donuts and coffee. Every day during her junior year of high school, when I was a senior, I picked her up for school with a bag of maple glazed and a white-chocolate mocha. It was a sugar shock to the system, that's for sure, but it never failed to make her smile.

I know that she works for the wild animal refuge just outside of town, so I park out front and, armed with all the sugar in the land, walk inside.

"We're not open to the public yet."

"I'm not here for the animals," I reply with a smile. "I'm hoping I can see Ally."

The man's eyes widen in surprise. "She's here, back with the babies."

"Can you please ask her if she has a moment?"

He nods. "Sure. Hang on."

He disappears through a door, and I'm suddenly as nervous as I was the other day when I rang her doorbell.

Here's hoping she doesn't pull a gun on me this time.

"Can I help—?" The words die on her lips when she walks out and sees that it's me. "What are you doing here?"

"I brought you breakfast." I pass her the bag and the cup of coffee with a smile. "I know you work super early and have already been here for a while, but I got a late start. Sorry about that. I hope you still like maple."

She frowns and glances into the bag.

"I haven't had one since the last time you..." She

swallows, shakes off the rest of the thought, and looks back up at me. "You left."

"No, you kicked me out. There's a difference. You don't have to go home, but you can't stay here." I wink and lean on the counter that she's standing behind. "I bought a house. I think you're going to like it. I hope so, anyway."

"You bought—?" Her mouth opens and then closes again. "What in the hell, Arch?"

"We can talk about it all later." I tap the counter with my palm and step back. "I shouldn't hold you up. Enjoy your breakfast. I'll pick you up at six."

"For what?"

"Dinner, of course."

I turn and whistle as I step out of the building.

I wasn't lying the other day. She used to make a hell of a spaghetti. But she always loved it when I made tacos. So, for tonight, that's precisely what I'm going to make her. It works out well because I can prepare the majority of it early, then go pick her up and finish it up when we get back to the house—after I've given her a proper tour of the place.

With all the veggies chopped and ready, the cheese shredded, and the pico and guac made and in the fridge, I grab my keys and hurry out to my car, ready to drive across town to Ally's house to bring her home with me. I'm craving her company. Bandon is a small town, but I can't get to her fast enough. After I park and take a deep breath, I walk up and knock on the door.

There's no answer.

I frown and knock again, then walk over to look in a window.

No movement inside.

I head around the house, and there she is, sitting on her deck with her feet up on the rail and a glass of wine in her hand.

"There you are."

"Go away, Archer."

"No way."

She rolls her eyes. "Is the fact that I don't want you here really that big of a hit to your fragile male ego?"

I know what she's attempting to do. She's trying to piss me off and push me away.

It's not going to work.

"I've told you for days, I'm not going anywhere. You don't want me to stay here, and that's totally fine with me. I would prefer to be able to hold you at night, but I can respect your wishes."

"Obviously, you can't, because I told you to go *home*."

"Well, technically, I live here now."

"Tell me you didn't actually buy a house."

"I did. You're going to love it."

"Archer."

"Ally."

She stumbles over the next words and frowns. "You called me Ally."

"That's your name, remember?"

She blinks quickly, the way she does when she's surprised.

"Listen, I don't care what your name is, as long as I get to be with you. So, yes, I bought a house, and I'm here to get to know you better. To get to know you *again*."

"This is a *very* expensive courtship," she says, swirling the wine in her glass.

"You're worth it," I counter. "Now, are you going to come let me feed you, or what? I have everything ready for you."

"I shouldn't," she says. "I should demand that you respect my wishes and go."

"No, you should come and see this killer house and eat my tacos."

"Tacos?" Her eyes fly to mine, and she swallows hard, tries to seem unimpressed. "I don't even like tacos."

I step to her, and without touching her, lean in to brush my nose over hers. "Liar."

"Tastes change."

"Not when it comes to tacos, sweetheart."

"Did you buy a house on the beach?"
"Yup."
"Tacos *and* an ocean view?"
I simply smile at her.
"Fine."

SEATTLE

7
~ELENA~

Until I rode in Archer's car the other day, I didn't realize how much I missed heated seats. Yes, it's a first-world thing, and I'm not proud of it, but it's true. My backside just sinks into the warmth of the leather, and I could live right here, for a long time.

He drives us along the beach and pulls into a driveway that ends at a three-car garage.

"Are you telling me that you just bought a seven-figure house because you want to *date* me?"

Seeing him walk into my job today was a shock to my system, almost as bad as the day he came to my door. I'd been so sad, so *lost* since he left the other night. I was sure I'd never lay eyes on him again, and I was in the process of grieving not only my grandmother but also the loss of Archer all over again.

And then I walked into that room and saw him

standing there, and it was as if everything in my world snapped back into place.

Which is crazy.

"Among other things."

I blink, confused. "Excuse me?"

"I bought the house because I want to date you, along with some other things." He unclips our seatbelts as the garage door lowers behind us. "Come on, I want to show you the place. And I'm hungry."

"You're always hungry."

He grins and pushes out of the car, hurrying around the hood to open my door before I can do it myself. He was always the type to open doors for me, and it seems that hasn't changed.

"It's better to walk through the front door," he says, opening the side garage door. "We'll just walk out this way."

"I'm sure it's fine through the mudroom."

"Next time. I want you to get the full effect this first time."

He takes my hand, linking his fingers with mine as if it's just second nature and not a conscious decision. The heat travels from my palm, up my arm, and settles in my shoulder, making me shiver in delight.

"Are you cold?"

I shake my head no and smile as he unlocks the door and leads me inside.

The view is incredible. I can see the rocky shoreline, the calm water beyond, and it takes me a second to catch my breath.

"Wow."

"I know," he murmurs, standing back with his hands tucked into his pockets as he waits for me to soak it all in. The view out the windows is beautiful, but the man before me is a complete shock to the system. He always was, even as a young man. But Archer in his early thirties? Holy shit. He's tall with broad shoulders and muscles in all the right places.

Sinew for days.

His hips are lean. And his abs? Well, let's just say if it were a hundred years ago, a girl could wash her clothes on his stomach.

"Keep looking at me like that, and my manners will fly right out that window, and I'll take you here on the kitchen counter, Elena."

Elena.

I quirk a brow.

"It's just the two of us, and I'm smart enough to never put you at risk out there." He gestures with a nod of his head in the direction of town. "But when it's you and me, you're Elena. I'll be damned if I'll say another woman's name when I'm being intimate with you."

"I never agreed to anything intimate." I lick my lips and will the damn butterflies in my stomach to get lost. "I agreed to tacos and a view."

"You'll get both." He reaches up and drags his thumb down my cheek. "And that's all. For now. Let me show you the rest of the house."

He leads me through bedrooms, bathrooms, and an office with a desk that's empty aside from his laptop. The house is big, much too big for one person, but it's comfortable.

"It's a lot of house."

"It's ridiculous," he agrees. "And the smallest one available with these views. So, I snatched it up."

"In one day?"

"I got lucky."

I give him a look that says *right*.

"I really did. The former owners moved out of state, and this was all staging furniture. So, I just bought it all."

"Just like that."

He walks behind the island in the kitchen and starts pulling bowls out of the fridge.

"Like I said, I got lucky." He sets a skillet on the gas stovetop and turns on the burner, then dumps some ground beef into the pan and starts to stir. "Not to mention, money talks, sweetheart. I made a pitcher of margaritas if you want one. I also bought that wine you like, if you'd rather have that."

I sit on a stool and stare at him. Am I dreaming? Archer is in Bandon. He bought a house and is making me tacos.

What alternate universe am I living in?

Whatever it is, I don't want to leave.

"I'll have a margarita. I wouldn't want them to go to waste."

"Good idea." He fills two glasses and clinks his to mine. "Cheers."

"Cheers."

He takes a platter out of a cupboard. Who knew serving implements would be part of the staging items included in the house? As he begins to pile stuff on it, the smells coming at me are amazing and make my stomach growl. I didn't realize I was so hungry.

"Let's take this all out onto the deck and watch the sunset while we gorge ourselves on guacamole," he suggests.

I haven't had a better offer in years. I hop up and help him gather all of the food and our drinks, and we make our way onto the deck, where a small table and chairs are set up, just big enough for dinner for two.

"I admit, this is pretty great," I say as I dip a chip in the guac and shove it into my face as I look out to the sea that's as calm as it gets tonight.

"The view or the food?"

"Both." I watch him as he chews and swallows, his Adam's apple bobbing with the motion. "You're stubborn, you know that?"

"Hi pot, I'm kettle."

"Archer, you *bought a house*. And not just any

home. You bought this insanely big house. You could have stayed at the resort for a hell of a lot less."

"I'm more comfortable here," he says with a shrug. "Besides, I've lived in a *lot* of hotels lately, traveling all over the country, trying to track you down. I'd rather have a home base for a while. And, after I'm done here, I can lease this place out and make some money. Flip it when the value goes up."

"How long did it take you to find me?"

"A few months."

I feel my eyes go wide.

"I couldn't just look for you every minute of every day. I had to go back to Seattle for blocks of time so I could work, be with my family, that sort of thing. But when I could get away, I returned to the search."

"Why now?"

"Because Anastasia screwed up and let it slip that she hears from you now and then. I didn't want to talk about it. But then she messed up more by admitting that she knew why you ghosted me after we got married. After that, I became a man obsessed. I had to find you. I mean, I took one night to get stinking drunk and sing bad Irish songs in Kane's brother's bar, but then I got down to business."

"You sang Irish songs?"

His lips twitch. "Not well."

"I wish there was a video of that."

"No, you don't. Trust me."

"I still can't believe that after all this time, you came to find me."

"You *married* me," he says, his voice suddenly heavy with impatience. "I vowed to love you for better or worse. And you up and broke it off so suddenly that you made my head spin. And you wouldn't talk to me. We were together for two years, attached at the hip, and then one day, you were just gone."

"I was trying to protect you."

He growls, and I reach over to lay my hand on his arm.

"Listen to me. You don't understand because I never talked about it much. I just wanted to be a normal girl with you. I didn't want to be the princess. Different. Being with you, with your family, was the most incredible experience of my life."

"So you left me?"

"You're not listening." I want to smack him. "I never told my family I was with you. Not after I tried, and my father told me to break it off. I knew it was too risky."

"Elena." He sits back and stares at me in surprise.

"You weren't from the right pedigree. You certainly weren't who my father would have chosen for me. So, I had to keep it all a secret. I stupidly thought that if we got married, if I went to them and said it was already done, there wouldn't be anything they could do about it. I figured they'd just have to get used to it."

He pinches the bridge of his nose. "Christ."

"My father was insanely pissed," I continue, flinching at the memory of my father's face when I told him. "I'd seen him angry before, of course. He was a scary man, especially when he was mad. But I'd *never* seen him like that." I shudder at the memory of those days. Of the beating, the whipping.

The branding.

"What did your mother think?" he asks, pulling me out of the horrible memories.

I frown. "It didn't matter what she thought. My father was the boss. And not just of the household, Archer, he was a mob boss. An insanely powerful man. If he wanted you dead, he would have done it in a heartbeat and wouldn't have lost a moment of sleep over it."

He finishes his fifth taco and pushes his plate away, then takes a sip of his drink.

"Did he still punish you?"

You have no idea.

I shrug a shoulder and look out at the water. Gulls fly overhead, and the bottom of the sun is just starting to kiss the top of the horizon. The sky is a riot of color, like a fresh bruise. Like the ones I wore around my eyes for days.

"Did he punish you?" he asks again.

I take a deep breath and let it out slowly. "Making me lose you was the worst of it."

Emotional pain is always worse than physical.

"What else did that fucker do?"

His voice is hard now. I glance back at him and let my eyes roam over his face, his eyes and nose, full mouth. Yes, losing Archer was the worst thing that ever happened to me in my life.

"It doesn't matter."

"It does to me."

I stand and walk to the railing and watch people walking on the sand below. Archer joins me. He's close but doesn't touch me.

"There's a code in the family. They don't physically hurt women. Punishments are psychological, and there were plenty of those over the years. I was usually a good girl, so the punishments were always small. But this was a pretty big deal, and I pushed him past his patience."

"What did he do?"

"Archer, it was a long time ago." And something I don't like to think about. Because when I do, I can feel the whip. I can smell my dad's cologne. I remember the helplessness I felt as I hung by my hands, and the despair when I realized that my relationship with Archer was over.

But that was long ago, and I have no plans to rehash it.

He takes my shoulders in his hands and nudges my

chin up to look me in the eyes. I don't want to tell him. It'll make him feel guilty and hurt all over again.

"I don't want to talk about it right now."

"Will you ever want to talk about it?" He steps back and shakes his head in disappointment. "We can't build a relationship on lies."

He tosses my own words from the beach the other day back at me.

"I'm not lying to you. I'm telling you, point-blank, that I don't want to talk about the shitty past. Can't we just enjoy this sunset and each other's company for a while? Can't we simply live in the here and now?"

He sighs, and his eyes soften. "For now. But not forever, Elena. I deserve the answers to my questions."

Despite the frustrating conversation earlier, the evening has been wonderful. An incredible sunset and even better conversation made the time fly.

If he asks me to stay tonight, I don't know if I'll be able to say no.

It feels too good being with him like this, in this amazing house. I could almost let myself daydream for a moment that this is *our* house. That we're married and living our life like ordinary people. The way it should be. The way it was *supposed* to be.

But that's silly, and I learned long ago that such daydreams are a waste of time and energy.

"What are you thinking about?" Archer asks after slipping the last dish into the dishwasher and snapping it shut.

"That I'm glad I came here tonight," I reply.

"I am, too. You look good, sitting here in my kitchen."

"You don't look so bad yourself."

His impossibly blue eyes narrow, the way they always did when he was feeling particularly sexy. I don't have to be a mind reader to know he wants me. The feeling is entirely mutual.

Maybe staying isn't such a bad idea.

"I should probably get you home," he says, surprising me.

"Oh. Right. Yeah, I should go."

He rounds the island and wraps one arm around my waist. His lips are inches from mine as he leans in.

"I want you to stay," he whispers. "Make no mistake, I want it more than I've wanted anything in my life. But it's too soon, and you have to work early tomorrow. When I have you, I don't want time constraints, and I don't want secrets between us."

Well, then.

I lick my lips and nod, watching his mouth as it pulls up in that cocky grin that always puts a knot in my stomach.

Archer reluctantly pulls away, and we make our way to his car in the garage.

The drive to my cottage is quick and silent, as both of us are lost in our thoughts. I'm suddenly bone tired. I feel like I could sleep for a week.

What is it about this man that exhausts me? And he hasn't even kissed me! Not really, anyway. The brushes of lips over breakfast and before he left don't exactly count.

"I like these seats," I murmur as I shimmy down into the warmth of the leather. "So comfortable."

"Don't fall asleep on me, sweetheart. We're almost there."

I smile and close my eyes, enjoying the warmth, darkness, and the sounds around me.

I feel him turn down my road, and then into my driveway.

"Thanks for the ride." I open my eyes and turn to find Archer watching me with a serious expression. "What's wrong?"

"I missed you, E. More than I even realized."

I reach for his hand and pull his palm against my cheek. "I missed you, too."

I kiss his skin, and then the moment is gone. Archer climbs out of the car and walks around to help me out. With our hands linked, he walks me to the door. The night has come awake around us with singing night birds and the buzz of insects. Even from this distance, I can smell the sea. The last of my summer geraniums are starting to wither.

"Do you want to come in?" I ask.

"Yes." He sighs and cages me in against the still-closed door. "So, I'd better not."

His eyes drop to my lips, and before I can say anything else, he cups my face and neck in both of his hands and lowers his head to mine, covering my mouth in the sweetest kiss I've had in more than a decade.

One hand slips down my shoulder, my arm, and lands on my hip. His fingers tighten, just enough to let me know he's there.

I can't help myself. I step into him, pressing closer, and surrender to the kiss. I want to lose myself in him. I want to remember what it feels like to be with Archer in this way. There's absolutely nothing better in the world than when this man focuses his whole attention on me as if I'm the only one in the world.

With a growl, he nips at the corner of my mouth and teases me with his tongue. But that's as deep as he takes it, and he backs away far too soon.

"You're as sweet as you ever were," he whispers against my lips. "Maybe sweeter, and I didn't think that was possible."

I swallow hard and, without giving myself time to overthink it, I wrap my arms around his middle and hug him close. This man was once my husband. He's meant more to me than anyone else in my life besides my grandmother.

And he's here.

And despite his words to the contrary, he's not leaving.

This could be catastrophic for both of us.

"Stop thinking so hard," he murmurs against my hair. "No one knows where I am. You're safe. *We're* safe, E. I promise."

God, I want to believe him.

He tips up my chin, and I stare into his gorgeous eyes.

"Trust me?" he asks.

"I've always trusted you," is my immediate response. It's true. Trust was never our issue. "But I don't know how you can trust *me* after everything that happened before."

"Stop beating yourself up, okay? I'll be just down the street a ways if you need me. And I'll see you very soon."

"How soon?"

"Tomorrow, most likely."

"Are you going to make a nuisance of yourself?"

"Oh, yeah." He laughs and kisses me squarely on the mouth, then steps off the porch. "You're gonna be sick of me before long."

I unlock and open the door, watching as Archer walks backwards to his car.

"I still think this is a bad idea."

"I told you, stop thinking. Sleep well, babe."

And with that, he gets into his car and drives away. But this time, I don't have a pit in my stomach at the idea of never seeing him again. No, now I'm filled with anticipation, wondering how I'm supposed to wait until tomorrow to see Archer. How am I supposed to sleep with the taste of him on my lips, and the thought of having his hands on me racing through my mind?

Yes, I want him, maybe even more than I ever did before. I'm no longer a girl wearing rose-colored glasses and telling myself lies of happily ever after.

I'm a grown woman, quickly falling in love once more with a man I've been tied to nearly all of my adult life. Being with him could literally be fatal for both of us.

This is a bad, bad idea.

SEATTLE

8

~CARMINE~

I had no idea that my grandmother was a hoarder. Admittedly, I didn't spend a lot of time in her home as an adult. As children, my brothers and I, along with Elena, spent weeks here in the summer, playing and exploring the big house on the cliffs. Nothing was off-limits to us.

Our grandmother doted on us the way any normal grandparent does.

The only difference was, ours was the matriarch of a mafia empire.

No big deal.

Cannonballs in the pool. Ice cream in the gazebo. Treasure hunts in the attic that spans the entire house, the space filled with antiques and trunks full of old things.

We loved being here together, where we could do

as we pleased and be indulged by a loving grandmother.

I miss her already. I was at her bedside when she died, the only one in the room when she whispered her secret to me.

"Elena," she said, making me sigh.

"She's not here, Grams."

"Helped her," she said and then coughed. "Helped her get away."

My eyes narrowed.

"Is she alive, Grams?"

"Hidden," she confirmed. "Find her before your father. Keep her safe."

And when I was carrying her casket at the church and looked up and saw the two different-colored eyes staring back at me, I *knew*. I knew it was Elena. She could wear any disguise in the world, and I'd still know her.

She was like a sister to me.

Of course, I had to tell my father that she's alive. If he found out I'd kept something that huge from him... well, I wouldn't like to know what the punishment for that might be.

But I played stupid about the rest of it. Grams knew that Elena was in danger, and I would find her and do everything in my power to keep her safe.

Now, to figure out where the fuck she is.

I've had a pit in my stomach for days. Rocco was

right in the elevator. There would be a punishment for her staying away from the family so long. For disregarding her place in the hierarchy.

The thought of it makes me sick.

I slam a desk drawer shut in disgust.

"I've been through here," I mumble, wiping my hand down my mouth. I've been over every inch of Grams' office.

There's nothing here.

On a hunch, I run my hand under the pen drawer and find a button. When I push it, an invisible drawer on the side springs free.

"Son of a bitch."

I look over my shoulder, even though I know for a fact I'm here alone. It's two in the morning. Rocco left several hours ago.

The drawer is deep and filled to the brim. I feel like a kid again, hunting for treasures in the attic as I start pulling things out and setting them on the desk before me.

A flash drive. That goes directly into my pocket. I'll look at it later from the safety and privacy of my own home.

A notebook full of nothing but numbers. No notes to explain what they mean, just rows and rows of digits. Could they be phone numbers? Bank accounts? I have no fucking clue.

I set it aside.

There's some jewelry, birth and death certificates. It seems Grams liked this hidden desk drawer for important things rather than an actual safe.

Which was empty, by the way.

A scrap of paper at the bottom of the drawer catches my eye.

I sit back and hold it up in the light.

Bingo.

I found her.

SEATTLE

9
~ARCHER~

"How was your day?"

I can't stop staring at her. We're in her little cottage, and she's gathering her things, a light sweater and her purse, almost ready to go out on our date. She's in a barely-there yellow sundress, perfect for the warm, late-summer evening. Her dark hair is loose and falls in waves down her back.

Southern Oregon is in the midst of an Indian summer. Or so I've been told at least six times today from various locals around town.

"Busy, but really good," she says with a smile. "We finally hired an extra person at the refuge, so I get tomorrow off. It'll be the first day off I've had in months, at least one that wasn't because of a funeral."

"Spend it with me," I say immediately and smile

down at her when her eyes jump up to mine. "Pack an overnight bag and spend the night at my place tonight. Tomorrow, we'll goof off together."

"I should get some things done. I have laundry and bills to pay. I was thinking about—"

"Please."

She sighs as if she's waging war inside herself, and then she turns without a word and walks upstairs to her bedroom.

When she's out of eyesight, I pump my fist in the air in celebration.

"I saw that," she calls down, making me laugh.

"You didn't see anything."

Less than three minutes later, she returns with the same overnight bag she took with her to Seattle. I toss it into the back seat of my car, get her settled, and pull out of her driveway.

"Where are we going?" she asks. "And am I dressed appropriately?"

"You're gorgeous." I head toward town. "I thought we'd do something tonight that we used to do back in the day."

She quirks a brow at me. "Did you?"

I feel my lips twitch. "Easy, tiger. For starters, we're going to a high school football game. It *is* Friday night, after all."

Earlier, I researched where the game is being held

so it would be easy to find. I pull into a packed parking lot once we arrive.

"Small towns *love* their Friday night football games," I say as I cut the engine and turn to smile at my girl. She's not smiling in return. "What's wrong? You used to love football."

"I still like it."

"My cousin Will will be thrilled to hear that."

She rolls her eyes. "I just don't usually come to these kinds of things. I try to blend, remember?"

"You're a member of this community. Going to a game isn't going to make you stand out like a sore thumb. Come on, it'll be fun. They have hotdogs, and I'm starving. Aren't you hungry?"

"For hotdogs?"

"They might have soft pretzels. Or nachos."

I waggle my eyebrows and get out of the car, then walk around to open her door and take her hand to help her up.

"So, it's a fancy date, then," she says while batting her eyelashes. "You shouldn't have."

"We spent many a Friday night at the football field when we were younger," I remind her as I link my fingers with hers and follow the crowd walking toward the gate.

"Yeah, because you were on the team, and I was a cheerleader. Attendance was required. Also, we were in *high school*. Here, we don't even know the kids playing." She stops short and blinks rapidly.

"What's wrong?" I look in the direction she's staring, but I don't see anything out of the ordinary. "What is it?"

"Nothing." She shakes her head and then smiles up at me. "I thought I saw something. Anyway, we're no longer *required* to come to high school games."

"Hey, it's football." I wink down at her, determined to have a good time tonight. "No pro teams in southern Oregon."

"True."

"Next!" a mom yells out. She's wearing a Bandon Tigers sweatshirt, a pin on her chest with a photo of a player, and gold and black paint on her face. My guess is she's the president of the PTA. "What can I getcha?"

"Four hotdogs for me," I reply and then look down at El—Ally. "You?"

"*Four*?" she asks and then shakes her head. "I'll have one hotdog and a Coke."

"Oh, a Coke for me, too."

The lady nods, shouts our hotdog order at the other mother filling those requests, and before long, we're paid up and walking away with our food.

The lights are bright overhead, and the sun is starting to set. The cheerleaders are at their post on the sideline, just inside a wooden fence, smiling for the crowd.

As we walk past, I feel Ally move closer to me. I glance down in time to see her narrowing her eyes at the girls.

"What's up?"

"Nothing."

We climb the bleachers and find a good spot, right in the middle of the crowd.

"For real, what happened?"

Ally takes a bite of her dog and shrugs a shoulder. "They were checking you out."

"They're like...sixteen."

She shrugs again.

"I don't go for jailbait, babe."

"You did once." Her voice is cool and matter-of-fact, and I can't help but bust up laughing.

"Yeah, over *you*. And if I recall correctly, I was also jailbait at the time, so it doesn't count."

She laughs now, and I finish off one dog in two bites, then start on the next.

"You know, this isn't a contest," she says, watching me. "You can chew it."

"I am."

"How can you afford to feed yourself?"

"Good thing I'm rich." I wink at her before taking a sip from the straw in my Coke. The game is about to start. A woman climbs the bleachers and sits next to me with a smile.

"Is this seat taken?"

"No, ma'am."

She lays a blanket on the bench, sits, then spreads another blanket over her lap like it's blizzarding out.

"Do you have a son playing?" she asks me.

"No, just here to enjoy the game. You?"

"That one." She points to the field. "Number two."

"Quarterback," I say with a nod. "Very nice."

"And that cheerleader," she continues, pointing to a blond girl in the middle, "is my daughter."

"Double the reason to be here," I say with a nod. "That's great."

"They're good kids," she says, watching her daughter as she laughs with a friend. "I'm a single mom, so it hasn't always been easy, but I have no complaints when it comes to them."

"That's great," I say again.

"So, not married, then?" she asks, looking at my ring finger. "Sorry, I'm Bea."

"Hi, Bea. No, I'm not married, but I'm here with my—" My what? Girlfriend? Ex-wife?

"I'm Ally," Ally says, reaching around me to offer her hand for Bea to shake. "And I can hear you."

"Oh, I was just making conversation," Bea says, clearly flustered. "I certainly didn't mean any offense."

"Of course," Ally says with a nod and sits back, mumbling under her breath, "Home-wrecker."

I lean over to whisper in her ear. "Your green eye is especially green tonight, sweetheart."

"Your blue eyes are both about to be black," she says with a saccharine-sweet smile. "Must you flirt with anything in a skirt?"

"To be fair, she's not wearing a skirt. And I wasn't flirting. I was *talking*."

"Hmph."

"You know, your jealous side always did turn me on. Seems nothing's changed in that regard."

Her eyes are pinned to the field, but her lips turn up in a half-smile. This is a conversation we would have had before. Teasing and easy. She's not easily swayed to jealousy, so I know she's just giving me shit —the way she always did.

Falling into an easy cadence with her is as simple as breathing.

The game is underway, Bea keeps to herself now, and I spend the next two hours cheering for a team that isn't mine, in a town that isn't mine, next to the woman that *is* mine.

"Come on, ref, put your glasses on!" Ally yells, almost coming off her seat. "What a jerk."

I grin down at her. "I knew you'd enjoy yourself."

"I'd enjoy it more if that ref knew what a decent call is." She shakes her head in disgust. "He's not a great banker, either."

"Excuse me?"

"The ref. He works at the bank."

"Small towns," I murmur with a smile, enjoying

myself. She's getting so worked up by the game, it's hilarious to watch. "You would love watching Will play."

"I've been," she says and sends me a sly smile. It fills my heart to know that she's still interested in my family after everything that went down between us. They loved her and were upset when we broke up. "I drove to San Francisco to watch him a couple of years ago. I always liked your family."

"I know." I swallow and watch the quarterback throw the ball. "They liked you, too. Still do."

She nods. "Anyway, it was fun to drive down for a couple of days and watch him play. He used to remind me of you."

"Because of the amount of food we ate?"

"That," she says, "and your personalities. You're both easygoing, funny. Kind of cocky."

"Hey, I'm not cocky."

She laughs and shakes her head. "Have you met you? You're completely cocky. But not in an asshole kind of way."

"Uh, thanks?"

She takes my hand in hers, smiles, and then resumes watching the game. I want to cover my heart with my hand and sigh.

I have it bad. Real bad. I don't know how we're going to make this work, but there is no other choice.

Because I'm not leaving Bandon without her. Next week or next month, I don't care when.

"You put in a hot tub?" she asks as she stares dumbfounded at the bubbling tub out on the deck. We stepped out to listen to the surf below. "That was fast."

"I work fast," I reply. "It seemed like a good investment. Who wouldn't like to sit out here in that tub, watching the ocean? If I end up using this place as a vacation rental, it'll help lure in vacationers."

"I would rent it," she says and dips her hand in the water. "Is it all ready to go?"

"Yep."

"I'll be right back."

She turns and disappears into the house. I want to go after her, but my phone rings.

"Hi, Stasia," I say.

"How's it going?"

"Great."

"Are you with her?"

"Yes."

She huffs on the other end of the line. "Gee, you're so talkative. Tell me things, Archer. Where are you? What did she say when she saw you? What are you doing now? When are you coming back to Seattle? Are you an item again?"

"Christ, do you ever stop talking?"

"I need information. You've been very tight-lipped. So, where did you find her?"

"I'm not telling you that."

She pauses. I can just see her face in my head, her brow furrowed in a frown.

"Why ever not?"

"Because she doesn't want anyone to know where she is."

"Well, you have to tell me *something*."

"No, I don't."

"What if something happens to you? What if something happens here, and I need to send for you?"

"Send for me? What is this, sixteen-sixty? I have a phone. Call me."

"Archer Steven Montgomery."

"That's not going to work, and you know it."

She sighs dramatically, and I can hear a deep voice in the background.

"He won't tell me where they are."

"Is that Kane?"

"Of course, it's Kane."

"Tell him to rein in his wife."

I grin and wait for the sputtering and spitting to come. I'd never have the balls to say that in person, she'd slice me in two, but from this safe distance, I can't help it.

"Have you lost your bloody *mind*?" she screeches, making me laugh loudly.

"You deserved it," I remind her. "We're safe, we're fine, and that's all you're going to get out of me."

"Stop hassling your brother," I hear Kane say.

"Listen to your husband, the way a good wife should."

"I'm going to slash all your tires when you get home."

"Goody. See you."

I hang up as Elena walks out of the glass doors, wearing nothing but a towel.

At least, I think it's nothing but a towel.

"Turn around," she instructs me.

"Hell, no."

She tilts her head to the side and raises a brow. "Do it, Arch."

I sigh and turn my back on her. "Fine."

I hear something fall to the deck, the water sloshing, and then, "Okay. I'm in."

I turn to see her submerged to her neck. She pinned her hair up, and she's resting against the headrest.

"This is divine."

My tongue is stuck to the roof of my mouth. She

shifts, exposing the tops of her breasts, and I feel my cock harden in response.

"You should join me. I won't look while you strip down."

I blink, giving it more thought than I ever figured I would. I want to jump right in and take her, right here and now. The image of us naked and slick, making love in that water is at the forefront of my mind.

But I didn't plan to take it there tonight. I mean, I *want* to. But I won't until she can be open and honest with me about all aspects of her life, not just her body.

"Archer."

"Yeah?"

"Get in the water. Before I'm a prune."

I don't ask her to turn away. I strip out of my clothes and sink into the water. I sit across from her, keeping my gaze steady on hers.

"Who were you chatting on the phone with?" she asks. A droplet of water drips down the side of her neck and runs down her chest to the bubbling surface.

I can't take my eyes off the wet path that droplet took.

I've never been jealous of water before in my life. I guess there's a first time for everything.

"Arch?"

"Sorry?"

She grins. "Phone call?"

"Anastasia."

All humor leaves her face as she stares at me from across the tub. "Are you kidding me?"

"She's my sister."

"Did she ask where you are?"

"Of course, she did."

"Shit."

"That doesn't mean I told her. Elena, I have to have contact with my family. It's my *family*."

"How could I be so stupid?" she mutters.

"Whoa. Hold up. Neither of us is stupid. But you're the one hiding, not me. If I don't stay in contact with my siblings, they'll put an all-points bulletin out on me, and all of the Pacific Northwest will be looking. I didn't give her any information."

"Someone can trace your cell phone. Why do you think I don't have one?"

"I turned off the GPS on my phone. I did it the minute I left Washington. But if the mere thought of me talking to the people who love me the most pisses you off, we need to figure this out now. I'll call in Caleb or Matt or *someone* to help. You can't just hide here forever."

"Stop it," she says, shooting daggers at me with her eyes. "You don't dictate how this goes, Archer. I've been doing this for a *long* time. You're right, I can't tell you not to speak with your sisters. That's not fair. But I won't sit here and be a sitting duck either."

"I'm telling you, you're safe."

"And I'm telling *you*, you don't know what you're talking about."

She stands in the dark and climbs out of the water, grabs the towel off the deck, and stomps inside. I hurry after her.

She slams the bathroom door shut and locks it before I can fling it open behind her.

"Open the door." My voice is way calmer than I feel. "Elena, you have to know that I'd *never* put you at risk, and neither would my family. We're not stupid, and we're not careless."

"You don't get it," she says when she steps out of the bathroom, clad in her dress once more.

"Then tell me." I don't let her rush away. I cage her in against the wall and tip her chin up so I can look in her eyes. "*Talk* to me, Elena."

"It would be easier if we just had sex and went our separate ways."

"I'm not sleeping with you."

That catches her attention.

"Well, that's a small blow to my ego, but I'll get over it." She moves to pull away from me, but I easily hold her in place.

"I'm not going to be intimate with you until you're willing to fully open up to me. I told you that already. Not until it's more than just this incredible chemistry between us. It's true intimacy. You're not just some girl I met at the gym, or the bar, or wherever. It's *you*, damn it. I need to know what happened twelve years ago. I *need* to know what they did to you."

She closes her eyes in defeat and leans her forehead against my chest.

"Archer."

My hands glide up and down her arms.

"Come on." She looks up at me now with clear, determined eyes. "Let's go outside."

"I'll pour us some wine on the way."

"We're going to need it."

Seattle

10

~ELENA~

I haven't gone back to that day in my head in years. The memory of the physical pain has lessened with time, and I always chalked it up to a lesson.

Once Archer has the wine poured, we take our glasses out into the dark evening. He covers the tub, and we sit in the plush chairs, facing the sea.

It's choppier out there tonight, just like the emotions boiling inside of me.

"I'm not sure where to start," I admit after I take my first sip of wine.

"The beginning is always a good place."

"Before I do, I need you to remember that this is the *past*, Arch. It can't be changed, and I'm fine now."

He blows out a breath. "Not ominous at all."

I lick my lips. "I was so happy that day you dropped me off at the house. The weekend in Idaho when we eloped was the best of my life, and I was riding high on that adrenaline. I didn't think anything could touch me. I figured I'd make my announcement, pack my things, and call you to come and get me."

"That was the plan," he agrees.

I sip my wine and lick my lips. "My father was… livid. I'd never seen him like that before. He reminded me of my place in the family and then dragged me up to my bedroom."

I methodically explain the next twenty-four hours to him. From the moment my father tied me up, to the phone call where I lied to Archer and broke off our relationship.

When I finish, he doesn't say a word. He simply stands and walks to the railing of the deck and stares out at the beach. The anger rolls off him in waves. His fingers white-knuckle the railing, and the veins in his forearms are corded and popping out. For me, it's old news, but for Archer…it's happening here and now. All I want to do is soothe him.

"I know it's hard to hear."

"Stop." He turns back to me and shakes his head. "It's not hard. It's fucking unbelievable. Inconceivable. Evil. Terrifying. I could go on."

"I get the idea."

He crosses to me and squats in front of me, his hands on the arms of the chair. He's not touching me.

"I want to see the scars."

"Archer..." I look at him and shake my head. "I don't know, I—"

"Elena." He grabs my hand, squeezing it tightly. "I need this. You were the love of my life, and I dropped you off and left you there."

"Don't try to take the blame. This is all on him."

"Please."

Without hesitation, I raise the skirt of my dress high on my thigh, where the *W* is branded on my skin.

"That son of a bitch." His voice is rough with emotion, but his fingers are careful as he lightly traces the scar. He leans in and gently lays his lips on the wound and kisses me there. "And your back?"

I stand to show him, but a light from the neighbor's house comes on.

"Inside," Archer says. "And don't let me forget to have a privacy screen installed."

He leads me through the house to his bedroom, turns on the sidelight next to the bed, and then turns back to me.

"Are you sure?"

"I'm going to kiss every inch of your amazing body before too much longer, so I'll see them eventually. But I want you to show me."

I turn my back to him and let the dress fall around my ankles, then pull my hair over one shoulder, exposing my back.

"Christ."

I know what it looks like. That many lashes leave a hell of a mess on a person's skin.

"How many?"

"Archer—"

"How fucking many?" he demands. His voice, still raw, isn't raised, but that doesn't make it any less powerful.

"Twenty."

I expect him to kiss them. Touch them. But he surprises me by simply wrapping his arms around my chest from behind and burying his face against my neck. *This* is what I needed all those years ago. *These* are the arms I needed around me, to reassure me, to hold me.

And we were both robbed of it. We lost so much time. We lost each other.

"Oh, baby. I'm so sorry I wasn't there. I'm so sorry I didn't fucking kill him myself."

"You were safe, and that's all that mattered to me," I insist, turning in his arms so I can see his handsome face, memorizing every line all over again. "This isn't your fault. You didn't do anything wrong."

"I failed you," he whispers. "I shouldn't have left you alone that day. I should have insisted that I go in with you to face him together."

"You wouldn't be standing here now if you had," I remind him. "And that would have destroyed me. I did what I had to do. And I'd do it again in a heartbeat if it meant keeping you whole."

He tips his forehead against mine.

"That's the whole story. You know everything now, Archer. My family is more ruthless than you could ever imagine. Every cliché, every rumor you've ever heard about the mafia is true, and in some cases, worse. They kill people, they run drugs. They hide money. They're bullies. But if you're part of the family, you're in for life. There's no leaving."

"You left," he reminds me.

"I escaped. And only because my parents were murdered, and my grandmother was worried that I would be the next target. I got lucky. But I don't know how long this is going to last for me."

"I won't let anyone touch you ever again," he pledges and brushes his lips over my chin, then up to my lips. "I'll keep you safe, Elena. I swear it."

"I've missed you so much," I admit. My heart rips open wide and feels so full of joy that he's here. "It terrifies me that you insist on staying, but God, it's so good to feel you. To talk to you."

"I told you, I'm not going anywhere."

His fingers draw light circles over my back, making my nipples tighten in anticipation of receiving the same attention. I push my hands up into his hair and hold on as he takes the kiss deeper and guides me back to his massive bed. He lowers me and then covers me with his hard body. He's familiar and new at the same time, filling my senses in new and exciting ways.

Archer and I were together sexually when we were young. Still, it didn't happen often, and only in the last few months of us being together. I was a good Catholic girl, and I was young. Archer was patient, and when we did finally have sex, it was sweet and loving. Innocent.

And usually, it was quick. Not because he had no stamina, but because of our schedules and our families. Getting caught was always a concern.

So, taking our time to truly explore each other never happened until our wedding night.

Three days later, it was over.

"Stop thinking so hard." His voice is rough with lust as he kisses down my neck. "Say the word, and this ends."

"Definitely don't stop," I reply with a grin and then sigh when his hand glides behind my knee and begins to make small, soft circles that trail up the inside of my thigh, making my pussy tighten in joy. "Oh, man, that feels good."

"Your skin is so fucking soft." His fingertip brushes over the *W,* and he pauses. "Look down, E."

"Huh?" I open my eyes and find him staring down at me with those gorgeous blue eyes.

"Look down," he repeats and glances down to my thigh, where he's tracing the *W* on my skin. "When we look down like this, it doesn't look like a *W* at all. It looks like an—"

"*M*," I say with him and feel the last knot in my stomach break free.

"Montgomery," he says, his grin cocky, and then kisses me once more before moving those talented fingers in toward the part of me that's been longing for him for a dozen years. "Ah, baby."

I gasp as his finger slips inside, and when he pushes a second one in with it, I feel the orgasm gather at the base of my spine.

"Archer."

"Yes, sweetheart. Let go. I'm right here."

I fall apart, my back arches, my toes curl. And he's there, murmuring sweet words and caressing my neck with his lips as I float back to Earth.

"I don't have condoms," he admits with a growl. "And trust me when I say, I want to punch myself in the face for not getting some."

I laugh and shake my head. "I've been on the pill for years."

His eyes light up again. "Yeah?"

"Oh, yeah. We're good."

He links our fingers and presses them into the mattress near my head. "Are you sure?"

"Archer, I'm gonna need you to get a move on here."

His lips twitch as he fumbles with his clothes.

Then he's braced over me once more, kissing me softly and thoroughly as he pushes in gently, inch by inch, until he's fully seated inside me.

"Christ Jesus, Elena. How is it better than I remember?"

"Because it's now." I lift my legs higher on his hips, opening myself to him even more. "And because it's right."

I don't even know how much sex I've had with Archer over the past few days. I'm quite sure it's more than all of the times we did it put together when we were young.

Maybe we're making up for lost time.

Or maybe we're creating memories to hold on to when he's gone, and I'm left alone again.

I frown at the thought. Of course, this isn't forever. It can't be. But I've resigned myself to simply enjoying every minute that I'm given.

I didn't stay with him last night. I was with him Friday and Saturday night, and I decided I needed a night away. Mostly, I was being stubborn and stupid because I was lonely when I woke up this morning.

And maybe a little moody.

Even my car didn't want to start. Probably because I didn't drive it all weekend.

But we're on the road now, on the way to work. Getting back to some normalcy will be good for me.

Run-down car, awesome job, Ally. That's who I am.

I nod and square my shoulders, but then my car decides to throw a temper tantrum. It sputters and dies. I'm lucky I can at least steer it to the side of the road.

"Well, shit." I lay my forehead on the wheel and contemplate my options.

It's early in the morning. The only people I know who are awake are my coworkers, who are currently *working.*

They won't be able to help.

And Lindsey is most likely at the spa already, getting ready for her first client at eight.

I pop the lever under the steering wheel and step out of the vehicle, lift the hood, and stare down at what looks like a heap of garbage to me. I don't have the first clue what any of this is, how it works, or how to fix it.

And I don't own a cell phone.

I blow out a long breath and look up and down the road. It's empty at this time of day.

"I just *had* to move to a small town," I mutter as I walk back to the driver's side door. But before I can open it, a familiar vehicle pulls up behind me. "Archer?"

He steps out, shuts his door, and walks toward me with a frown. "What's wrong?"

"I have no idea. It died." I kick the tire and then curse myself as pain shoots through my toes. "Pile of junk."

"Did you call a tow?"

"No phone."

"Right." He pulls his cell out of his pocket and taps the screen, then places a call. "Hi, I need a tow truck."

His eyes are on mine as he tells the person on the other line where we are, what kind of car it is, and then hangs up.

"Thirty minutes," he says.

"You don't have to wait. I'm sure they'll give me a ride to work. I'll have to figure out how to rent a car around here."

"Why? You have me." He leans a hip against my car and looks mildly annoyed.

"Yes, because I'm sure you want to be at my beck and call, driving me all over town. You're not a chauffeur."

"You go to work, and you go home. It's really not a big deal. I'm sure they'll have this fixed in a couple of days. No need to waste money on a rental."

"Really? *You're* going to tell me what I should and shouldn't waste my money on, mister I bought a whole *house* so I could *date*?"

"That's completely different."

I roll my eyes and lean on my car, my arms crossed over my chest.

"Oh, can I borrow your phone to call my job and let them know I'll be late?"

He passes me the mobile and waits while I do just that.

"Hey, Chad, it's Ally. I'm going to be late. My car broke down."

"No problem. Be safe."

"Thanks."

I hang up and pass the phone back to Archer.

"Appreciate it."

"I didn't like sleeping without you last night," he says and links his fingers with mine, then pulls my hand up to his lips. I was trying so hard to put a little distance between us, to not let myself go all mushy when it comes to him, and then he does stuff like this. "I didn't sleep well at all. So, I was going to fetch your breakfast."

"Do you mean you were going to get *yourself* some breakfast and get me some at the same time?"

"Well, sure." He smiles down at me. "A man has to eat."

I laugh and lean my cheek on his biceps, relieved that he was here to help me this morning. His muscle feels firm and warm against my cheek. "Thank you."

"Come stay with me for a while."

My head whips up. I stare at him as if he just asked me to jump off a bridge.

My stomach flutters as if he did just that.

"What?"

"You heard me."

"Why would I do that?"

He shrugs a shoulder. "Because I'm irresistible? Because you can't stand being away from me? Because I'll cook you all the tacos you want and rub your feet and eat your—"

"Point taken."

He gives me a wicked grin, and I feel it all the way to my center.

"I have a home," I reply slowly.

"Well, you don't have a car for a few days."

"We don't know that. Let's find out what the garage says."

"Two weeks."

I stare in shock at the man with *Lee* written on his coveralls.

"Excuse me?"

"It'll take two weeks," he repeats. "That part isn't one we keep in stock, and I'm backed up since my nephew up and left town with the girl he knocked up this past spring. So, unfortunately, your car is gonna have to wait."

I sigh deeply.

"That's if you want to fix it," he continues.

"Why wouldn't I want to fix it?"

Lee looks down at the paper on his counter. "Well, it has almost three hundred thousand miles on it. This week it's the fuel pump, but next week, it'll be the alternator or something else. It's lived its life."

"I'm not putting my car to sleep," I mutter. "Please, fix it."

"Yes, ma'am."

I give him my information, grab his card so I can call him later, and walk out with Archer. He was unusually quiet the entire time we were in there.

"Just say it."

"You need a new car, babe."

"That one will be just fine."

He shakes his head. "If you're worried about standing out, just buy another used car. It doesn't have to be fancy, but it does have to be reliable. You don't carry a phone. I found you on a deserted road, alone, at oh-dark-thirty. It's not safe."

"This one will be fine," I repeat. I know I'm being stubborn. I don't care. "Thanks for the ride to work."

"What time should I pick you up?"

I start to tell him *no thanks*, but when he looks at

me, his eyes tell me he's at the end of his patience with me today.

And I'm too tired to argue.

"Two should be fine."

"Two, it is."

I nod and sit back in the warm leather seat. Being driven in this luxurious car for a couple of weeks won't be a hardship. We're passing through the heart of town when I see the same black Mercedes SUV that I saw in the parking lot of the football game the other night.

Black with tinted windows and black rims. Just like my father used to drive. What is a car that cost that much money doing in Bandon, Oregon?

Is it the family? Are they here, looking for me? Or is it just a coincidence? This *is* a resort town, and people come to visit from all over.

That's the logical answer. But I don't like it.

"And then we got new mountain lion cub triplets," I say as Archer drives me home from work. "They can't be more than three weeks old. Absolutely adorable. We don't know where their mama is. Probably poached."

I feel the heat creep up my face. Whenever an animal is lost to the greed of humans, it pisses me right off.

"Why people feel the need to illegally kill animals is beyond me. There are seasons for hunting, for the love of Moses. But we'll take care of them. The goal is to release them back into the wild."

"That's pretty incredible," he says with a nod. "I'm glad it turned out to be a good day. Now, about moving in with me."

"It feels silly to do that."

"Why?"

"Because I have a home."

"Yes, but if I'm going to be your chauffeur, it makes sense that you base out of my place until the car is fixed."

"It's not that I don't enjoy being with you, or even *want* to be with you. I hope you know that."

"But?"

"But it feels fast, and it feels like I'm taking advantage of you."

"You're not. There, we solved that problem."

Okay, he does make a good point. And, frankly, I missed him last night. And didn't I decide that I was going to enjoy every minute with him that I could get?

"You're awfully sure of yourself."

"I'm just positive that I want to be with you. If you'd rather I move into the cottage, I can do that. I don't mind."

"It seems like a waste to not stay in that gorgeous beach house," I reply.

He pulls into my driveway as I bust up laughing. But the laughter dies when I see my front door standing wide-open.

"I'm going to assume you closed that when you left this morning."

"I always double-check the locks," I confirm as dread spreads through me. "They found me. Oh, God, they found me."

"Don't jump to conclusions. And stay put." He pulls out his phone and dials 911. His hand reaches for mine as he waits for someone to answer. "We believe we have a break-in."

He rattles off my name and address, and within five minutes, the cops show up.

There's been no movement inside.

I get out of the car, but the officers motion for me to stand back.

"We're going to do a sweep, make sure no one is in there. Then we'll get your statement, miss."

"Of course."

Archer moves up beside me and wraps his arm around my shoulders as we watch the cops go inside and around to the back of the house. Less than two minutes later, they reappear, holstering their weapons.

"There's no one here, but someone definitely ransacked the place."

Bile rises in my throat.

"Can I go in?"

"Yes, ma'am. We need you to tell us if anything is missing."

There's only one thing of value in there.

I run inside and up to my bedroom, wanting to sob at the sight of my little cottage. I hurry to the dresser, open the bottom drawer, and breathe a sigh of relief when I see the photo of my grandmother, exactly where I put it days ago.

Whoever was here, they didn't find it.

But the rest of my place is in shambles. Furniture turned upside down, cabinets open, drawer contents spilled. It's a disaster.

And it's going to take days to clean it up.

"I don't know if anything's been taken," I say when I step back outside. "It's too much of a mess to know off-hand."

The officer nods and passes me a card. "Call me anytime if you discover anything's gone. We've had a string of auto theft in the area, and my guess is they're getting braver. Especially since your place is secluded."

He nods, shakes Archer's hand, and then both officers leave.

"I'm going to throw up."

"Hey, hey, hey," Archer says, rubbing a big circle over my back. "It's going to be okay."

"I have a bad feeling, Arch. I think it's the family."

"We don't know that. You heard him, it's probably

kids. You need to gather up a few things and come home with me. I have a state-of-the-art security system, and no one even knows I'm here."

I nod in agreement. "Thank you. I think I'll take you up on your offer."

"Come on. Let's get you home."

SEATTLE

11

~ARCHER~

She's been sitting on the balcony with her knees drawn up to her chest, watching the sea, since we got home two hours ago. She's hardly said a word. Her dark hair blows around her face in the breeze, and her expression is sober.

But I can see it in her gorgeous, unusual eyes.

She's scared.

And that pisses me right the fuck off.

"Here's some tea." I set it on the wide armrest of the chair and sit next to her.

"I'm not sick," she reminds me and tries to offer me a smile.

"It's just tea, E." I can't help but touch her. Maybe I need the reassurance as much as she does. I reach out to link my fingers with hers and give them a squeeze. "You heard the officer. It's probably kids."

She doesn't touch the mug. Doesn't tear her eyes away from the water. But her fingers tremble in mine.

"I have a bad feeling," she says as she takes a deep breath and lets it out slowly. "A very bad feeling."

"Hey." I pull her out of her chair and settle her in my lap, kiss her temple, and cuddle her close. "You're safe here, E."

She doesn't reply. She just leans her head on my shoulder and continues watching the water.

"What would you normally do after work?" I ask.

"Run errands, maybe go to lunch with Lindsey. Perhaps try to get a walk in at the beach."

"You should take that walk. It'll help."

She looks at me now and then kisses my cheek. "Do you mind if I go alone?"

I don't want to admit that I'd prefer that she go alone. I have some things to do, and I'd rather she wasn't here when I do them.

"I don't mind at all. Enjoy your walk."

She stands and takes a sip of her now-cold tea. "Thanks for this, too."

"You're welcome."

"I won't be long."

"Take all the time you need."

She doesn't have to go back inside to get shoes or a jacket. She just jogs down the staircase that leads to the sand and takes off to the south, toward the rocks we ran to together.

I take a moment to watch her, and then I walk inside to my office, sit at the computer, and make a phone call.

"This is Montgomery."

"This is also Montgomery," I reply to my cousin, Matt. "Bad time?"

"I'm home today," he replies. "What's going on?"

"Is your line secure?"

He's quiet on the other end for a moment. I hear him walking, then the sound of a door closing.

"How secure do you need, Archer?"

I pinch the bridge of my nose, already regretting this call. Still, I trust my relatives implicitly, and I need information. It's handy having a police detective in the family.

"Arch?"

"Yeah." I clear my throat. "I need some information, and I can't tell you why I need it."

"That's not really how this works."

"I know. Matt, I found Elena. Let's just say what I need to know involves her family, and if they were to find out that I was looking, or trace me to where we are, it could be incredibly dangerous for her."

"What do you want to know?"

"I need to know what their movements have been. Specifically, if they've traveled out of state. And if so, where."

"Archer, traveling isn't against the law."

"But you could look, without alerting them."

"I'll see what I can do. Archer, be careful. This family isn't warm and fuzzy. They're ruthless. And they're sneaky as fuck. Maybe you should leave Elena where you found her and get on with your life away from the damn mafia."

"If it was Nic, would you walk away?"

He sighs hard on the other end of the line. "No. I wouldn't."

"Didn't think so."

"I'll let you know what we find, but it'll be a few days. I want to make sure we do this right, and on the down-low, so low that no one can detect it. If it's done any other way, it could put my men's lives at risk. I'm not willing to do that, not even for you."

"I wouldn't ask you to. Thanks."

"Why now, Arch? What happened?"

I don't know how much I should tell him. The less he knows, the better. "Someone broke into Elena's house this morning. Ransacked it. Local cops think it was kids, but I want to make sure there's no chance that her family is in town."

"Understood. I'll look into it. Be careful."

He hangs up, and I sit back in my chair, staring out at the water. Elena would be livid if she knew what I just did. But I have to know, and I trust Matt a hell of a lot more than I put faith in the cops here.

"I'm finally getting spaghetti out of you."

I lean my shoulder against the fridge and watch as Elena chops up an onion to add to the ground meat sizzling on the stovetop.

"I figure since you're driving me all over, and letting me stay here, it's the least I can do."

"You don't have to repay me," I reply and watch as she dumps the onion in with the meat. "You'd do the same for me."

"Maybe." She shrugs and then grins at me. "Okay, probably."

"Are we having garlic bread with that?"

"Of course. And Caesar salad."

"You're a goddess."

She barks out a laugh and stirs the pan. "The old cliché of charming a man through his stomach sure is true with you."

She adds sauce and seasonings. Garlic. Gives it another stir, then covers the deep pan.

"It needs to simmer for a bit," she says.

"Good."

I move in fast, turn her to the wall, and pin her there as my mouth ravages hers. The desire, the all-encompassing need for her never ends. No matter how many times I have her, it doesn't appease the fire I feel for her.

Her mouth is eager under mine, matching me nip for nip. Her hands are in my hair, fisting and then combing, then clenching again.

I move in closer, glide my hands down her sides to her ass and then lift her. She wraps those gorgeous legs around my hips, and I grind against her, making us both moan in pleasure.

"Need you," I whisper against her lips. I push her hands over her head and pin them there while I continue kissing her senseless.

"No."

"Yes."

"No, Archer." She wiggles out of my grasp and pushes against my shoulders. "Let go."

I set her down and blink rapidly as she hurries away from me across the kitchen and wraps her arms around her middle.

"Whoa, what just happened?"

She clamps her eyes shut and whispers, "Shit."

"I'm gonna need you to talk to me, babe." I carefully step toward her. "If some asshole hurt you—"

"No, it's nothing like that." She shakes her head and pushes her fingers through her hair in agitation. "It's just the whole having my hands pinned above my head thing. It gave me a bad moment. And I know that's not fair to you."

"What a mean son of a bitch," I growl as frustration and rage fill me all over again.

"Without question," she agrees.

"I wish he hadn't died," I admit and prowl around the living space. "Because I'd like to rip him limb from limb until there's nothing left of him. What right did he have to treat you like that? You're his *daughter*."

"I was his possession," I remind him. "And, yes, he was mean. Ruthless. Feared. And my mother? Well, I don't know if she was worn down so far by that time that she had no fight left in her, or if she really didn't care about me at all. I don't remember ever receiving a kind word or affection from either of them.

"But if someone else tried to mess with me? They were dealt with. So while they didn't love me and couldn't be bothered with me most of the time, if push came to shove, they had my back."

"Out of principle, but not because they loved you." Anger rages inside me. Elena is sweet and kind. She always has been. How could they *not* love her? "Obviously, because he tortured you for marrying someone you loved."

"To them, obligation and love were the same thing." She huffs out a breath and walks to me. "I'm not afraid of you, Archer. I don't think you're going to hurt me. I just had a bad moment when you had my hands over my head. It was a gut reaction that had nothing at all to do with you."

"I want to hurt them for hurting you," I admit

softly and finally reach out to drag my fingertips down her cheek. "I want them all to pay."

"They did."

"All of them."

She shakes her head. "My cousins, my uncle, they were always great. I don't know how my father had so little emotion in him, but his brother-in-law, my aunt's husband, was always loving and fun. He has a great sense of humor, and he was always fair. I loved him. I grew up with his three sons as if they were my brothers. They didn't do anything wrong."

"And yet, you're running from them."

She frowns and looks down. "Because I have to. Even if they love me. And I, them. The fact that I fled the family doesn't change. There will be hell to pay if they ever find me. The punishment won't go unfulfilled."

"And what do you think that punishment will be?"

"Death."

"You already said they don't physically harm the women in the family."

"Not my death." She swallows hard. "Yours."

"They don't know that I'm here."

"It doesn't matter. They know that, no matter what over the years, you've been the one thing in this life that means the most to me. Father made me leave you and promise never to pursue you again. And he swore, that you—your life—would always be the thing the family held over my head for the rest of *my* life. Or yours."

"So, I'm the pawn used to hurt you."

"If you want to put it like that."

"That's not okay with me. I'm a grown man, and I can fight my own battles."

"Not against them." She sits, her face lined with worry. "You can't win against them, Archer. But they don't matter as long as they don't know where I am."

I pull her to me and wrap my arms around her, holding her close. "They won't find you."

"Enough of this," she says and pulls back to smile up at me. "I have dinner to finish. You haven't eaten in about three hours. You must be starving."

I smile for her benefit. "I'm withering away over here because someone's holding out with her spaghetti."

She laughs, plants a kiss on my chin, and walks away.

"This will be ready in fifteen minutes."

I don't have the heart to tell her that I'm not hungry. For the first time since I can remember, it's not food that I want at all.

It's revenge.

SEATTLE

12

~CARMINE~

I haven't seen her yet.

But I know she's here.

"Can I get you another glass, sir?"

The waiter smiles, gesturing at the glass of wine I've been sipping for over an hour. I shake my head.

"No, thank you."

"Dessert, then? We have a delightful lemon cream cake with strawberry compote, or the house tiramisu, which is always a favorite."

I haven't had a good tiramisu since I was in Italy last year. My sweet tooth wants to beg for a slice.

But I have a job to do, and indulging in sugar isn't part of it.

"I'll just take the check, thanks."

"Of course, sir." He pulls a leather folder out of his pocket and lays it discreetly on the tablecloth. "Whenever you're ready."

He walks away from the table, and I sip what's left of my wine. I know Elena's here. I can feel it in my bones.

But I haven't seen her yet.

It's only a matter of time.

A text pings through on my phone.

Shane: *Any luck?*

Me: *Not yet. With no name to go by, it's not easy to ask around. I'll give it one more night, and then I'll start showing her photo around town, see if that turns anything up.*

Shane: *She might not be there. This could be a waste of time.*

Me: *She's here.*

Shane: *How do you know?*

Me: *Call it a hunch. I'll be in touch tomorrow.*

I slip enough cash for the bill and a substantial tip in with the check and slide it away from me. I take one last sip of my wine and stand to go back to the hotel for the night when a woman with dark hair and the right height walks into the restaurant. I can't see her face because she's walking away from me, but I'd swear it's Elena.

Same shape. Same hair. Even the gait of her walk is the same.

My blood hammers through my veins as I walk toward her. She's with a man, about the same height as my six feet, his hand resting on the small of her back as he escorts her to their table.

The host seats them, her back still to me, of course, and then passes them menus. I wait for him to leave and approach, catching the man's eye.

I ignore him and look down into blue eyes.

Not green and brown.

Blue.

"Can we help you?" the man asks.

"My apologies," I say, shaking my head as I glance down at the woman who is most definitely *not* my cousin. "I thought you were someone I know. Enjoy your evening."

Fuck.

I walk out of the restaurant and turn toward the hotel. The town is so small, there's no need to drive anywhere. I thought finding Elena would be easy in such a tiny community. But after two days of looking, that's proving to be false.

And every minute that I don't find her only irritates me more.

It's past time for my cousin to come home and claim her rightful place with the family.

Whether she wants to or not.

SEATTLE

13
~ELENA~

The window's open. I can hear the water churning below and the seagulls' calls as they fly overhead, searching for breakfast.

I reach my arms over my head and push against Archer's tufted headboard, stretching sleep away. I'm quickly getting accustomed to these Saturday mornings off work. It never really bothered me to work every day, but sleeping in once in a while has its perks.

One of the benefits is morning sex. But when I roll toward Archer's side of the bed, I'm met with cool sheets instead of his warm body.

I open my eyes and sit up, pushing my hair back to glance around the spacious bedroom then out to the deck.

He's not there either.

I pad naked into the bathroom, and once I've

brushed my teeth and used the facilities, I pull on a pair of shorts and a T-shirt then go in search of Archer.

There's still time for a morning romp.

I grin at the thought. When we were younger, morning sex wasn't something we could indulge in. We never lived together, despite being legally married for just shy of a week.

But now, sex is on the table any time of day, and in the four days I've been staying here, we've taken advantage often.

It hasn't quenched my thirst for him. If anything, the regular sexcapades have only made me want more.

I've turned into a wanton woman. Well, where Archer's concerned anyway.

I swing by the kitchen that's quickly become my favorite room in the house, aside from the perfect balcony where I sit and watch the ocean, and fill a glass of water.

I can hear thumping coming from downstairs, so I follow the noise.

I turn a corner, and there he is, in the workout room, punching a bag that hangs from the ceiling. He's shirtless, wearing only a pair of grey sweatpants that look as if they've been through war. At some point, he cut them off just above the knee. The drawstring is pulled and tied, keeping them low on his hips.

That V that women go on and on about? Yeah, it's

there. Along with a six-pack that would make the gods weep.

I lean against the doorjamb and sip my water as I watch him beat the shit out of that bag. I wonder who he's picturing in his head as he throws the punches.

Whoever it is, he's cleaning their clock.

I'd ask him, but he has earbuds in. So I settle in to watch.

He stops punching and, to my amazement, immediately falls down into the push-up position, easily pumping out twenty reps as if it's nothing at all. He's breathing hard and sweating like crazy, but his body moves with such fluidity that he makes it look easy.

His muscles bulge as he moves from push-ups to a hanging bar, where he executes ten pull-ups and then turns back to the bag.

Jesus.

Who knew? I mean, his incredible body is obvious. I've been with him, naked, several times now. I've touched him everywhere. I *know* what he looks like.

But watching him go through the motions that help to keep him in stellar shape does things to my already overstimulated libido.

So, I set the water on the hardwood floor just inside the door and strip out of my clothes. The motion must catch his eye because he turns my way, breathing hard, sweaty. His eyes narrow on me.

He pulls the buds out of his ears and tosses them

aside just before I dash to him and jump against him, wrapping my legs around his waist as I clamp my mouth to his.

"Whoa," he says in surprise and stumbles back, but catches himself and sits on a bench with me situated on his thighs. "Good morning."

"Fuck me." I bite his bottom lip and scoot back on his legs to tug at the drawstring of his sweats. "Right now."

"Never was good at telling you no." He grins and helps me work his shorts down his hips. When he springs free, I pump him twice with my fist before rising up and lowering myself over him, making us both moan in delight. "Jesus, babe."

"So hot," I chant as I ride him, fast and hard. "So fucking hot."

I'm clenching around his hard length. I can feel the orgasm building in me, the power that flows whenever we're together like this. I don't want to slow down. I don't want to stop.

I want to make him lose his mind.

He pushes a hand between us and presses his thumb against my clit. I can't hold back any longer. I explode around him, crying out as I shiver and grind down. To my delight, he pulls me against him hard and comes, as well.

We're a panting, writhing heap.

It's fucking glorious.

"Hi," he says and kisses my collarbone.

"Hi, yourself."

"What happened?"

"Saw you working out."

His bright blue eyes fly to mine. "That's it?"

"That's all it takes, champ."

His lips twitch as I pull away and stand, freeing him from the bench.

"And why is that?"

"Do you need me to stroke your ego?"

"You already did that." He tugs up his shorts and ties the drawstring.

"Okay, look." I pull my T-shirt on and prop my hands on my hips. "You've always been hot. Like, stupid hot. You were so good-looking that it was almost unfair."

"Keep going." He grins, his arms crossed over his chest, clearly delighted by this conversation.

"Somehow, you're better-looking now than you ever were. And I don't know how that's possible. Like, did you sell your soul to the devil or something?"

"No."

"I'm not complaining. I want you to know that this is *not* me complaining, not in the least. But I don't understand it. It's a mystery. Anyway, you've only managed to improve with age, and then I came down here looking for you and found you doing"—I wave my arms around—"this."

"What?"

"Punching the hell out of that bag, and push-ups like they're your job. And *that*." I point at the pull-up bar. "With your back muscles flexing and everything."

"So, you like it when I work out."

He tips his head to the side, watching me.

"Yeah." I swallow hard and nod once. "Yeah, I do."

"Good to know." He grabs a towel off a shelf and wipes down his face and neck. "I've been training pretty hard with Ben in Seattle. It's how I'm able to eat pretty much what I want and not gain a gut."

"Who's Ben?"

I watch his Adam's apple bob as he takes a drink of water.

Damn, I have it bad.

"You've been gone a long time," he says, but there's no censure in his voice. "I'll give you the CliffsNotes version. My cousin Jules married Nate. Nate's dad owned a gym in downtown Seattle, but he recently retired, and Ben bought it. Ben is Matt's wife's best friend."

I blink at him, not following at all.

"I'm gonna need a diagram. I think your family tree is more confusing than mine."

"There are days I need a diagram, too."

"Well, whoever Ben is, I like him."

"I can't believe you've never been here," Archer says later that evening. We're sitting in the dining room at the resort's restaurant. It sits on the cliffs, looking out over the Pacific Ocean. We have a window seat where we can watch the birds and sea life below.

"I came to the resort for a massage a few years ago," I reply and sip my crisp white wine. "That's how I met Lindsey. But I've never had a reason to come up for anything else. Certainly not a fancy dinner."

"The steak's good."

I grin. "My salmon was great, too."

"I know." He eyes the last of my apple pie. "I stole a bite when you went to the restroom. Are you going to finish that?"

"Yes." I eat the pie and watch as his eyes round and then look sad. "Aw, poor guy."

"It's okay, I'll take some home for later."

We don't hurry. When more wine is offered, we accept it and linger over the candlelight and conversation.

"How are your parents?" I ask, realizing that I haven't inquired about them before this.

"Good," he says. "Dad had a heart attack last year. Gave us a scare. But he's recovered, and Mom has him eating mostly rabbit food, much to his dismay."

"I always liked them," I murmur. "I'm glad that everyone is doing so well and that your dad recovered from his heart attack."

I regret not being there for Archer during what I know was probably a terrifying time.

"Why did you sell your fishing boat?"

He sips his wine. "I was offered a *lot* of money from one of the bigger operations. I was sick of spending the majority of the year at sea, away from the family. It was time to be a land dweller, and real estate always interested me."

"We used to spend hours driving past places for sale," I say, remembering back. "And going on that Parade of Homes, daydreaming our way through gorgeous places."

"I still do that," he says. "I love what I do now. It's not nearly as smelly, the income is steadier, and I'm around for the family whenever they need me."

"You always did take care of everyone around you, Archer. Even me." I finish my wine. "You're still taking care of me, it seems."

He looks like he's about to say something, but we're interrupted.

"Hey, guys." Lindsey grins as she approaches the table. "I didn't expect to see you here."

"I could say the same about you," I reply. "You don't usually work this late."

"I had a late client, and then I had some inventory to do. Being the boss sucks sometimes." Her gaze shifts between Archer and me, but I don't offer any information.

I know I'll get drilled later.

"So," Lindsey says, "Archer didn't leave town, after all."

"Nope," he says with his charming grin. "Ally decided she wanted me to stick around for a while."

"He's like the plague," I reply. "He just never goes away."

Lindsey laughs. "Must be nice, having someone so handsome sticking close."

"Don't make his head any bigger than it already is."

Lindsey's cell rings, and she checks it. "Sorry, have to take this. Have a nice dinner."

She waves and hurries away to take her call.

"She'll insist on lunch soon so she can ask all the nosy questions that friends do." I watch as Archer signs his name on the receipt. "Which is fine. She's a good friend."

"I'm glad you have someone here. I hate the thought of you being alone."

"I have Lindsey and my coworkers, who are all great. I have a fulfilling life here, Arch. I'm not sad or bored."

"I'm glad."

The waiter brings out to-go boxes full of desserts, and we stand to leave. As we walk out the door to the parking lot, Archer's phone rings.

"Hello? Yes, she's right here."

He passes the cell to me, just as a car catches my eye. It's the black SUV. A man is in the driver's seat, but the windows are tinted enough that I can't see his face.

And the license plate is from Washington.

My stomach jumps into my throat.

"Ally?"

I look up at Archer. "Yeah?"

"Phone's for you."

"Oh, right." I take it from him and fumble with it before pressing it to my ear. "This is Ally."

"This is detective Garcia. I wanted to update you on the case. We arrested two suspects today. When we found your iPad in the backpack of one of the boys, they confessed to the break-in and robbery of your house."

"Wow." I blink at Archer as he holds the car door open for me. "Thank you so much. I didn't even realize my iPad was missing."

"It had your name on it," he says. "Inside the cover."

"That's mine. I appreciate your work on this, detective."

"You can pick up the iPad at the station anytime."

"Thank you."

I hang up and sit in the car, then pass Archer his phone.

"Good news?" he asks.

"It was kids, after all." I fill him in on what the detective told me. "So, yeah, good news."

"That's great."

He starts the car and pulls out of the parking space. The SUV is gone.

Part of me knows I'm being ridiculous. This is a *resort*. People vacation here from all over the place, including Washington. In fact, it's *likely* someone from Washington would come here because it's within driving distance. It's probably a family who came down for a long weekend at the beach.

That's what common sense tells me.

It's most likely *not* someone from my family in their typical mafia-style vehicle, looking for me.

The odds of that are incredibly slim.

But the odds aren't zero, either. And my gut says something's coming.

My instincts are rarely wrong.

Summers at Grandma's are the best. I get to come here with my cousins—Carmine, Shane, and Rocco—and we can do whatever we want for two whole months.

The servants keep our pantry stocked with our favorite snacks. The treehouse has been mended and remodeled over the spring, ready for us to wreak havoc in it, pretending to be pirates or knights of the round table.

We can play down at the beach during low tide, searching for treasures.

And in the evenings, we have movies and popcorn until we fall asleep.

We look forward to it more than Christmas. More than anything.

"Come on, Elena," Carmine calls, gesturing for me to follow him. Carmine is the oldest—and the smartest. I love all of my cousins, but Carmine is my favorite. He lets me tag along almost anywhere.

The other boys get tired of me.

Carmine never does.

"Where are we going?"

"It's a surprise," he says and stops to wait for me to catch up. He takes my hand and leads me down a path in the woods next to Grandma's house. "You know I'd never let anything bad happen."

"I know, but what if there are bears? Or tigers?"

"Tigers don't live in North America," he says and holds a branch out of my way so it doesn't smack me in the face. "But if we see a bear, I'll fight him off."

I laugh at him. "Right. Like you could fight a bear."

"Hey, I've been working out." He flexes, showing me his fourteen-year-old muscles. "And no matter what, I'll always keep you safe, Elena. The family won't let anything happen to you."

"My father might," I admit in a small voice. "He's not very nice."

"*Does he hit you?*"

"*No.*" *I shake my head and shiver when the sun slips behind a cloud, making the woods cold. "No, he just says mean things sometimes."*

"*My dad says your dad's an asshole," Carmine admits. "I overheard him. At least you can always come here with us. And you can be away from there for a couple of months."*

"*This is the best time ever," I agree. "I'm getting tired. Where are we going?"*

"*Almost there."*

His hand tightens around mine as he leads me into a clearing. Suddenly, I'm not a child anymore. I'm a woman.

And in the clearing is scaffolding with a hanging rope.

Archer stands behind the rope with his hands tied behind his back.

"*What's going on?" I demand, staring up at Carmine. "What are you doing?"*

"*He's taking your punishment," Carmine says grimly, staring up at Archer. "For running from us. For staying away."*

"*Grandma—*"

"*Is dead," Carmine says, cutting me off. "She can't protect you anymore."*

I stare in horror at the man I love. His blue eyes are full of sorrow as he mouths, I love you.

I love you, too, *I mouth back.*

"*Please don't do this, Carmine."*

"It's already done."

He flicks his hand, and suddenly, Archer's neck is in the noose, and he's hanging, jerking about.

"NOOOOO! No no no no!"

I run toward him, but it's pitch-black now, and I'm falling. Falling and falling. Into what, I don't know.

"Archer!"

"He's not here," Carmine whispers in my ear. "He can't save you, Elena. Only we can. Only the family can help you."

"The family is a disease," I stammer as I cry out. "And I want nothing to do with it."

I sit up, dripping with sweat. Cool air blows in through the window and across my skin.

"Baby," Archer says, kissing my cheek. "It's okay. It was only a dream. You're safe."

"I need some water."

"I'll get it."

"It's okay." I kiss his cheek and then hurry from the bed, anxious to get out of the bedroom and away from Archer. "I'll be right back."

I snag my robe off a chair as I walk out to the kitchen. I pull it around me, tighten the belt, and rather than stop at the sink, I keep walking out to the deck to lean on the railing of the balcony.

I can't see the water. There's no moon tonight.

But I can hear it, and it soothes me.

I take several deep breaths, willing my heart to

calm down. Archer was right, it was only a dream. He's alive and well, and so am I.

Everything's fine.

I hear the door behind me, but I don't turn to him. He slips his arms around my waist from behind and kisses the top of my head.

"Wanna talk it out?"

"No." I turn and bury my face in his chest as I wrap my arms around him, holding on with all my might. "I just need you to hold me. Out here, like this."

"For as long as you need, sweetheart."

SEATTLE

14

~ELENA~

Margie, my boss at the wildlife sanctuary, is never at work when I am. She comes in to relieve me, working the swing shift.

But when I'm only halfway through my day, the woman comes walking into the nursery, dressed for work.

"Am I being fired?" I ask, wondering what in the world she's doing here.

"Hardly," Margie says with a laugh. "I just got this place fully staffed, and you're a dream. You'd better not be going anywhere."

"Then why are you here?"

She smiles in a way I've never seen before, confusing me more. "I'm giving you the next four days off."

I blink, sure I've heard her wrong. "Why?"

"Now that, I can't say. But from right now until Tuesday morning, you're off. With pay, I might add."

"Did I win the lottery?" I wonder, glancing around. "Hit my head on something hard? Is this dementia, and I just don't know it?"

"Follow me," she says, laughing at me. She leads me to our locker room where we keep our personal things and clean clothes.

Baby animals love to pee, poop, and throw up on people.

I stop short and frown. "What are you doing here?"

Archer grins that cocky, self-assured smile that never fails to hit me square in the gut.

"It's a surprise."

I inhale sharply, remembering those were the same words Carmine used in my dream last night.

"What kind of surprise?"

"This is where I go," Margie says and winks at me. "Have a great time."

She leaves the room, and I turn back to Archer.

"What's going on?"

"We're getting out of here for a few days. Away from Oregon and all of the ghosts that haunt you here. We need a vacation, babe."

"So you just arranged it with my boss?"

He rocks back on his heels. "I did."

I feel the smile slide slowly over my lips. No one's ever done something like this for me before. Maybe he's right. Perhaps a little holiday is exactly what we need.

"Where are we going?"

"That, my beautiful travel companion, is a surprise. But I already packed your bags, and Lindsey is going to keep an eye on your house. We're good to go."

"Wow. So, you're just whisking me away right this minute?"

"I can't figure out if you're excited or mildly pissed."

"I'm not pissed," I say with a shake of the head. "And depending on where we're going, I might be excited. So, tell me."

He moves in, wraps those ridiculously strong arms around me, and kisses me until I'm breathless.

"I'm not spilling the beans," he whispers against my lips. "And we'd better go before we miss our flight."

"Do I get to double-check your packing skills?" I ask as he guides me out of the building to his car.

"Nope."

He tucks me inside the vehicle and walks around to the driver's side, then climbs in and leans over to kiss me again.

This one makes my toes curl.

"What if I need something you forgot?"

"There are stores where we're going," he says as he

drives away from the sanctuary, and away from Bandon. "Don't worry, I've got you."

"You brought me to the boonies," I say seven hours later. We landed in a remote part of Montana, although I would guess that all parts of Montana are remote. Archer rented a Jeep Wrangler, and the late summer weather is nice enough to take the top off.

Mountains rise up all around us, the trees covered in varying shades of yellow and green leaves, contrasting beautifully with the deeper shades of the evergreens.

"Cunningham Falls," I read as we drive into a small town nestled next to the mountains. "How in the world did you find this?"

"Some of my family has talked about coming here to visit," he says casually. He's in ripped jeans, a black T-shirt, and aviator sunglasses. The wind blows through his dark hair, and he hasn't shaved in a couple of days, leaving a little scruff on his face.

He's damn hot.

"And before you yell at me," he continues, "no, I didn't call anyone and tell them this is where I am. I made all of the arrangements myself. Literally *no one* knows where we are. I told Margie I was just taking you away for a few days. No details."

He grins and pulls my hand up to his lips, nibbling on my knuckles.

"You went to a lot of trouble."

"It's no trouble to spoil you a bit," he says. "I wanted to be able to do this for you for as long as I can remember. But we were in school, and I was poor. Now, I'm not."

I sigh, feeling the weight of my situation lift from my shoulders for the first time in *years*. We're hidden, alone, and in this beautiful place for several days.

"I don't remember the last time I could really relax," I reveal and tip my face back to soak in the warm sun. "And I have to admit, it feels amazing. How did you know this is what I needed?"

I open my eyes in time to see him send me a look that says, *really?*

"You're coiled so tight, always worrying, always afraid that you'll be found. I can give you a few days of letting go of that worry." He drives us through a cute little town filled with shops and restaurants and then heads out of town and up a mountain road.

"We're not staying in town?"

"No, ma'am. This is a ski resort town. We're staying up on the mountain. I've been told the views are incredible and that where we're staying is world-class."

"Well, I can't wait to see it."

I don't have to wait long. After a couple of turns off

the main road that leads to a small ski village, Archer parks beneath what appears to be... "Treehouses?"

"Luxury treehouses," he says with a grin.

"Welcome!" We turn and look up to see a pretty blond woman waving from a deck above us. "I'm Jenna."

Archer waves, and we grab our bags out of the back seat and climb a staircase to one of the three treehouses. Jenna waits for us at the top of the stairs.

"I'm so glad you made it safely," she says. "I have you in the Ponderosa, which is on the end here. You'll have views of the ski run, the village, and after sunset, you can see lights from the town below.

"But the best part is at night. There's so little light noise here that you'll be able to see the stars in a way you never have before. The weather's been great too, so the show will be spectacular."

"Sounds awesome," Archer says and smiles down at me.

"Anyway, I'm babbling," Jenna says with a laugh as she unlocks the unit and leads us inside. "Sorry, it's been a long day. My number is here on the counter, along with the Wi-Fi information and anything else you might need to know. There are no other guests in the other two units right now, so you have the place all to yourself."

"We love the sound of that," Archer says.

I can't stop staring at the gorgeousness of this

place. The furniture is simple but inviting. The kitchen has blue cabinets, and the backsplash is in the shape of mountains. The beds look soft and cozy, and Jenna wasn't kidding about the views.

"This is stunning," I say at last.

"Thank you," Jenna says. "It's been a labor of love, that's for sure. You guys make yourselves at home and let me know if you need anything."

"Food," Archer says immediately. "We've been traveling all day, and I'm starving."

"He would be starving if we hadn't been traveling all day," I inform her, making her laugh.

"I have two brothers and a husband, I get it," Jenna says. "My favorite restaurant in town is Ciao. It's the best Italian food I've ever had."

"Perfect," Archer says.

"I'm going to freshen up," I say and smile at Jenna. "Thank you for your hospitality."

I walk through the master bedroom that's on the main floor and into a bathroom that makes my girlie-girl heart sigh in pleasure. The bathtub is deep and inviting. The separate shower is big enough for a party of six. And the décor of this place is absolutely on point. I'd call it rustic chic. Perfect for the mountains, but not *too* rustic.

I open my bag and am pleasantly surprised to see that it looks as if Archer thought of just about everything.

Except pajamas.

I smirk and unpack, choose a red summer dress to change into for dinner, and sweep a little makeup on my face before returning to the living room.

"I think I'm starving, too," I say when I join Archer, who's checking out the provisions in the kitchen. He glances up at me, and his jaw drops.

"Fuck me, you're gorgeous."

Every girl should have a man in their life that looks at her the way Archer's looking at me right now.

"You're not so bad yourself."

He walks around the kitchen counter and frames my face in his big hands as he kisses me, lightly at first as if he's memorizing the shape of my lips, and then he sinks into me, enjoying me. My head spins, and my fingers dive into his thick hair. But before I know it, he comes up for air.

"If I don't stop now, we won't eat, and I need my strength so I can do a hell of a lot more than this later."

"I like that strategy." I nip at his lips once more and then pull out of his arms. "Let's eat."

Jenna didn't steer us wrong.

"Okay, this is pretty great," I say after we order our food and have a chance to soak in the atmosphere. Our waitress wrote her name on the white paper on our table with an orange crayon. She just delivered wine and the best garlic bread I've ever had in my *life*. "If we had this in Bandon, I'd weigh four hundred pounds. And I haven't even had the entrée yet."

"This bread," he says with half a piece in his mouth. "I could die."

I love that we can sit here and enjoy ourselves, and I don't have to worry about being recognized by anyone. I don't have to even think about what my name is or if I'm in danger here. I can just be myself, a woman in love with this incredible man who brought me here on a surprise vacation.

And, yes, I'm in love with him. I can't deny it. He was wonderful when he was twenty, but he's absolutely marvelous now. I don't know how this will all shake out, but I'm going to enjoy him for as long as it lasts.

We've both earned it.

"You're gorgeous in red," he says before shoving more bread into his mouth. He doesn't eat like a Neanderthal, but he definitely enjoys his food. And I can't blame him. "You should wear it more often."

"So noted."

Our food is delivered, and the aroma of red sauce hits my nose and makes me want to moan in delight.

"We might have to move here," Archer says grimly after taking his first bite. "I don't know if I can live without this now that I know it's here."

"Okay, now you're just being dramatic." But I take my first bite, and my shoulders sag. "You're right. We're moving here."

The sun has gone down by the time we leave Ciao, our bellies full of the most amazing food. The tiramisu we ordered was the best I've ever had, and I'm Italian.

"I wonder why I didn't think to move here when I was looking at places to go," I say after I boost myself up into the Jeep. "It's kind of perfect."

"Because you love the ocean," Archer says as he starts the vehicle and pulls out of our parking spot to head toward the treehouse. "But now that we know this is here, we'll visit often."

"Deal." I settle back in the seat with a smile when a vehicle catches my eye. I freeze.

Late-model black SUV with tinted windows.

What in the actual hell?

My heart kicks up, and I want to panic. Did someone follow us here?

But I take a deep breath and force myself to push it aside.

No one followed us. No one knows we're here.

Am I always going to react this way whenever I see a black SUV? Maybe. But I need to learn to trust myself, and Archer.

We're safe.

The drive up the mountain is a little nerve-wracking in the dark, but we're soon back at the treehouse. A note is taped to the door.

I pluck it off and carry it in with us.

I hope you enjoyed dinner! There's a little something fun waiting for you out on the deck. Have a wonderful weekend,

Jenna

"The suspense is killing me." I walk over to the sliding glass door and pull it open, then smile when I see the hot tub open, and a standing ice bucket with champagne nestled inside. There is a small table beside the bucket with two flutes and a bowl of fresh strawberries. "I wonder if all of Jenna's guests get the royal treatment."

"I wouldn't know," Archer says casually as he strips out of his clothes and sinks into the tub.

"Uh, you're naked," I remind him.

"And I hope you'll join me," he says.

"We're outside. I'm not exactly an exhibitionist."

"There's no one here," he reminds me. "We're all alone. So, get naked and come in."

How can I resist him? I don't want to. I quickly shed my dress and slip into the water. Archer pours the champagne, passes me a glass, and before I can take a sip, he proposes a toast.

"To us, making new memories together."

"To new memories." I sip the bubbly and sit back in the tub with a happy sigh. "I'm travel weary. It wasn't easy to get here from Bandon. But man, was it worth it."

"I'm glad you think so," he says and looks up. "I don't think I've ever seen so many stars."

I follow his gaze and feel my eyes round.

"Wow. Jenna wasn't lying about this either."

It seems like the stars are so close, we could just reach out and touch them. The blanket of black is bigger than I've ever seen it before, with millions of stars winking at us.

"Jesus, it's beautiful," I whisper.

"Magnificent," he says, but when I glance his way, he's staring at me, not the stars above.

"You always were a charmer."

"I'm not trying to charm you." He sets his glass aside. "I'm only being honest. You're unbelievable, and I'm so fucking grateful that I found you."

He pulls me closer to him as the water bubbles around us, sending up steam and a cocoon of intimacy we've rarely shared before.

He leans in and presses his lips to the apple of my cheek. "I can't leave you. Not now that I've found you, Elena. I'd regret it for the rest of my life if I walked away from you, not after everything we've shared."

I want to protest, but I can't because the thought of losing him again sends absolute panic through me.

I shift, straddle him, and with my pussy pressed against the length of his cock, I cup his face and kiss him like I'm starved for it. His hands grip the globes of my ass, and he holds on tightly as I explore his mouth. The timer on the tub ends, extinguishing the bubbles, but the night around us sings, just like the blood pumping through my veins as I take the kiss from hot to inferno in the blink of an eye.

I move back and forth along his length. I want nothing more than for him to slide inside of me and take us over, right here and now.

What sounds like footsteps or limbs breaking pulls us out of our reverie, and the next thing I know, Archer pushes me away from him, his jaw hard and his eyes shining.

"It's just an animal or something," I say, moving back in, but he shakes his head, and I hear two people whispering.

"People going for a walk," he murmurs. Before I know it, he's standing, holding me up in the cool air. My skin is hot, not just because of the warm water but because my blood is moving fast through my veins. He easily maneuvers us out of the tub and into the house.

"We're dripping all over the floor."

"I don't care," he says and carries me through the house to the master bedroom.

"We can't lie on the bed all wet like this," I insist.

"No problem." He bypasses the bed and sets me

down on a chaise lounge that sits by the big windows that overlook the resort. He pushes the blinds so the moonlight still shines in, but no one below can see inside.

The moon is full, casting a glow over us. The droplets on our skin are starting to dry.

He stops kissing me and just pulls me to him, hugging me tightly.

"I said, don't stop," I mutter against his chest.

"I need to slow down," he replies and kisses the top of my head. "I want to savor every inch of you."

Before I can reply, he urges me back against the soft cushion of the chaise. I expect him to kiss me, but instead, he reaches for the pins holding my hair and pulls them out one by one until the long locks spill over my shoulders.

"I always loved your hair. You used to wear it shorter."

"I never have time to get it cut," I admit. "And I dye it darker myself. Just in case."

"I like it," he says and leans in to lightly kiss my lips. "I'm going to make you forget your own name tonight, Elena."

"Who's Elena?"

His lips, pressed to my neck, curve. "Exactly."

And here, in the moonlight, we rediscover each other all over again. His hands are bold and warm as they travel over my body. I can't help but arch into his touch and sigh every time he finds a sensitive spot on my flesh.

Every time is like the first time with him. It's the most incredible thing I've ever experienced.

"So responsive," he whispers before pulling a nipple into his mouth. He tugs gently and then scrapes his teeth over the nub. "So delicious."

"Killing me," I mutter as his hand roams down my belly to the promised land.

"You're slick." His voice is tight now as his fingers dance between my folds, sending me into a frenzy. "God, babe, you make me crazy."

"Archer." I can't breathe. I can't think. I can only feel this need inside, building until it feels like it's going to drown me. "Now, Archer."

He drops to his knees beside me, opens my legs, and replaces his fingers with his mouth. I almost jack knife off the chaise and come so fast and hard, I see stars.

He sets my leg on his shoulder and feasts on me. There's no other word for it. He gorges himself like a man starved, and it's so damn good, I think I might die from it.

When his hand glides down my leg and brushes over the scar on my thigh, he stills. When his eyes capture mine, they're slits.

"I'm okay," I assure him and push my fingers

through his thick hair. "I'm more than okay. It's an *M*, remember?"

He doesn't say a word as he stands, lifts me, and turns to the bed.

"Damn right, it's a fucking *M*."

I lift a brow. "Possessive, are we?"

"That hasn't changed, sweetheart."

But everything else has changed. His body, his voice, even the way he looks at me. He isn't a young adult anymore.

He's a man. A sexy, funny, irresistible male.

And he's kissing his way up my torso. His hands are in my hair, his elbows planted on the bed at my shoulders as he rubs his nose over mine, and his cock nudges its way inside me.

"Fucking hell." He shudders. "Ah, babe, you're incredible."

"It's us," I say and feel another orgasm gather. "It's us."

SEATTLE

15

~CARMINE~

"Excuse me." I motion for the bartender's attention and offer her a nod when she looks my way.

"What can I get you?" she asks.

I've been through more wineries and vineyards today than I care to remember, showing Elena's photo to everyone.

So far, no luck.

"I was wondering if you know this woman." I pull the picture out of my breast pocket and hold it out for her to see. "She's my cousin, and I'm looking for her."

She frowns. "Oh, sure. This is Paige. Paige Williams, right?"

Jackpot. I smile and nod as if I knew that was her name all along.

"Paige is a sweet girl. But she moved away some time ago."

And just like that, my joy falls flat.

"Moved away?"

"Yeah, it was the oddest thing. She'd been working here for a couple of years. Never missed a day of work. And then, one day, she just up and left."

"Do you know where she went?"

"Sorry, no. Never heard from her again." She looks me in the eyes. "If she's your cousin, why don't you know where she is?"

"She's been estranged from the family. Our grandmother recently died, and she's entitled to an inheritance. I'm just trying to locate her."

"Oh." Her shoulders loosen. "Well, I hope you find her. Sorry to hear about your grandmother. I should get back to work."

She walks away, and I tuck the photo back into my jacket and walk outside. Anger and frustration bubble up inside me. I just spent three days here, and it was all a waste of time.

I get into the car and immediately call my brother.

"She's not here, Shane." I fill him in on what the bartender said. "I was so sure. This was the only clue in Grams' house."

"I have a theory," Shane says. "I think we've been attacking this from the wrong angle."

I narrow my eyes. "Go on."

"What was the most important thing in Elena's life?"

"Just spit it out, Shane."

"Archer, Carmine. Archer was the most important."

"Uncle Vinnie put a stop to that."

"Do you really think they stayed apart all these years? If you were in love with someone so deeply that you were willing to go against a family like ours to be with her, would you stay away?"

"If Pop threatened to kill her? Yeah, I'd stay away. But it's an interesting theory. The only problem is, Archer's in Seattle."

"Not lately, he hasn't been."

My hand tightens on the steering wheel. "Keep talking."

"We're not sure where he went, but he's been out of the area for a while. I think it's worth looking into."

"You're the tracker in the family," I say, hope taking root in my belly. "Get looking."

SEATTLE

16

~ARCHER~

My eyes are blurry. If I didn't know better, I'd think I was coming off a bender with a hangover the size of Canada.

But, no. I didn't even finish that one glass of champagne last night.

I did, however, stay up most of the night making love with Elena. We might have snagged two total hours of sleep.

I'm not complaining. I waited a dozen years for this. Every minute with her is a gift.

I send up a silent thank you when I spot the Keurig on the countertop with a round carousel of different varieties of coffee pods.

I open a cabinet in search of mugs and lift a brow when I see Jenna's collection.

"How's that coffee coming?" Elena asks as she

pads up behind me and wraps her arms around my stomach, pressing a kiss to my shoulder.

"It's just getting started. Do you want *I'm no cactus expert, but I know a prick when I see one* or *Please cancel my subscription to your issues*?"

"Huh?" She leans around me to see what I'm looking at and lets out a laugh. "Oh, these are awesome. I have some funny mugs, but this collection is impressive."

"I think I'm gonna use *Hustle Juice*," I say, pulling the mug down.

"I love this one," she says, pointing to a mug on the second shelf. "*I think I've seized the wrong day.* Hilarious. Oh! *I don't like morning people. Or mornings. Or people.* This one is for me today."

"You like me," I reply with a sleepy grin as I pull that mug down and place it under the coffee machine, slip a pod in, and press brew. "According to last night, you like me *a lot.*"

"I like you and maybe four other people," she says and leans back against the counter as we wait for our coffee. She's in the black T-shirt I wore yesterday. Her hair is down and tumbled from a night of my fingers diving through it. Her legs are bare, along with her pink-colored toes.

Those fascinating eyes are heavy-lidded and full of satisfaction as she watches me.

"What are we doing today?" she asks.

"I thought we could go for a hike, if you're up for it."

"Are there bears here?"

"Possibly." I pour cream into her coffee and pass her the mug. "But I have bear spray, and there are enough people on these trails that I would be surprised if the bears hang out here. They're deeper in the woods."

"You hope," she mutters. "Because the one who runs the slowest is the bear food, and I can outrun you, my friend."

"Then you have nothing to worry about." I doctor up my coffee and kiss her lips lightly before walking past her and out to the deck where the hot tub and refreshments from last night are still on display. "I guess this sort of went to waste, huh?"

"No, it didn't," Elena says as she walks out behind me. "It did exactly what Jenna intended for it to do. It was romantic and sexy, and led to a fun-filled night."

After I close the lid on the tub, I sit on one of the deck chairs and tug Elena into my lap, careful not to spill our coffees.

"You're right." I nuzzle her ear and grin when I feel her shiver. "Are you cold?"

"It's a little brisk this morning," she says but then chuckles. "But, no. It's just you. Isn't it crazy?"

"What's that?" I brush my fingers through her

hair, watching the dark strands as they fall over her shoulder.

"When we were young, we had pretty good chemistry. I was young and very naive, but I knew it."

"You weren't stupid."

"I guess it's interesting to me that, all these years later, the chemistry just picked up where it left off. Except now, it's in overdrive."

"The heart knows what it wants, E, no matter how old it is."

She doesn't say anything for a long moment, she just sips her coffee and watches the birds fly between the trees. The mountain is waking up around us.

"It's going to be a great day for a hike," she says at last, signaling that our deep conversation is tabled for now.

Which is fine with me. We have plenty of time to pick it up again later.

"So, let me get this straight," she says an hour later when we're on our way up the trail that leads to the summit of Whitetail Mountain. "We have to hike *up*, and then we ride the chairlift down?"

"That's right."

"Why don't we ride up and hike down?"

"Because it'll be more satisfying to be able to say you slayed this mountain. It's only four miles."

"Straight up," she murmurs, but then stops to catch her breath and looks out at the view of the valley below. "Wow. The views up here are gorgeous."

"It's just going to get better the higher we go."

She sets off again, a few steps ahead of me. She may complain about the hike, but she's doing an awesome job of keeping a regular pace, stopping to drink her water, and catch her breath.

"You're a pro at this," I say.

"Hardly. But it is really pretty up here. Please tell me I'll be rewarded with something at the top."

"I've been told the view is incredible, and there's a restaurant where we can grab lunch."

"Awesome."

We pass several people along the way and encounter others who are on their way down.

No ride on the chair lift for them, I guess.

It takes us less than two hours to reach the summit, and we are not disappointed by the views when we get there.

"Holy shit," she breathes, her hands on her hips as she looks at the mountain range surrounding us. "I think we can see all the way to Canada from here."

"We can," I confirm. "I did some research before I booked the trip. Canada is due north. And to the east is Glacier National Park."

She just stares in awe at the snow-tipped peaks and the vastness of the trees and mountains in front of us.

When we turn around, we can see the valley below, with Cunningham Falls nestled against the mountain, right next to a large lake.

"This is seriously cool," she says. "It's also a good thing that I'm not afraid of heights. Are you going to feed me now?"

"That's usually my line." I take her hand and lead her to the summit house, the building that holds not only the restaurant but also a bar and a gift shop.

We place an order and choose a table inside to take a break from being in the sunshine, sitting next to the windows that look out to the mountains.

"We didn't see even one bear," Elena says as she adjusts her ponytail and takes in our surroundings.

"Told you."

"And how did you get me hiking shoes? In my size. On such short notice?"

"I called Jenna last night," I reply. "Gave her your size and told her what I had planned for today."

"You're just full of surprises," Elena says with a grin and leans back when our food is delivered. "Don't touch my onion rings."

"I wouldn't dream of it."

She narrows her eyes at me as she takes a bite of

her burger and then sighs in delight. "So good. I was starving."

"Hiking a mountain will do that to you."

Watching Elena eat is one of my favorite things to do. She enjoys every bite, and she isn't afraid to order exactly what she wants.

We don't say much as we inhale our food, and then make our way out to the chair lift to ride back down to the village.

"Oh my God," she breathes as we come over the side of the mountain and see the view spread out before us. "I don't know if I've ever seen anything quite like this."

"Now I know why the family loves it so much," I agree. "Maybe we'll have to buy a place here."

"You mean *you*."

I glance down at her and see she's shaking her head.

"You mean *you'll* have to buy a place here. I can't buy anything."

I sigh and wrap my arm around her shoulders. "Elena. You're a part of my life again, and I have no intention of letting you go. Ever. Whether you're Ally or Elena or another name, I don't care. I plan to live a life with you."

"Why?" Her voice is quiet. She stares straight ahead, but I don't know if she sees the magnificent view in front of her or if she's lost in her mind and the memories there. "Why would you risk everything for me?"

I tip up her chin so I can see her eyes.

"Because I'm in love with you. I've been in love with you for the better part of fifteen years, E. You're it for me. So, I'm going to do whatever the fuck I have to do so I can be with you."

Her chin wobbles, tearing me apart.

"Ah, baby. Don't cry."

"This could be so dangerous for you."

"*Not* being with you is dangerous for me." I kiss her forehead. "We don't have to have the answers today. We'll take it day by day and figure it out."

"You make it sound so simple."

"It doesn't have to be complicated." I kiss her temple and breathe her in. "I love you, E."

"I love you, too. I always have, Archer."

I want to shout from the mountaintop in joy.

Instead, I kiss her until my head swims.

We reach the bottom of the lift and walk the half-mile to the treehouse.

"I need a shower," Elena announces when we walk into the cool rental. Thank God for air conditioning on warm days like today.

"Go ahead," I say. "I'm going to grab some water. I'll be behind you."

She nods and walks into the master suite. I do

fetch the water, but I also make a call for dinner reservations.

When I walk into the bathroom, the mirror is steamed up. I strip out of my sweaty clothes and cast them aside.

"I didn't figure you'd want a super-hot shower after that hike."

I open the glass door and grin when she turns a soapy head my way.

"The breeze on the way down was cool," she says. "What are you doing?"

"I'm gonna check you over for ticks."

She scrunches up her nose. "That's disgusting. You didn't say anything about ticks."

"Don't worry, I'm here to save the day." I reach up and help her rinse her hair. "Have I mentioned how much I like your hair?"

"Once or twice." She lets her arms fall to her sides and leans into my hands as I massage her scalp and rinse the soap away. "That's nice."

It's about to get better.

When her hair is free of shampoo, I let my hands roam over her slick, wet skin. The scars on her back and thigh ignite the anger in my belly, but I take a deep breath, content to know that she's safe with me now.

No one will ever touch her again.

My fingers glide up between her thighs, and she sighs as she braces her hands on my shoulders.

"I don't think I have ticks there," she says.

"I'm just being thorough." I pick her up and slip inside her easily, as if she were made just for me.

Because she fucking was.

I brace her against the tile wall and fuck her hard and fast until we're both spent and weak.

"Water seems to be our thing," she says when I've set her back on her feet. "Good to know."

I smirk and stick my head under the spray of water. "Everywhere is our thing, babe."

"True." She smacks my ass with a loud *thwack*. "I'm getting out of here before you attack me again."

"You're not going to wash my hair for me?"

"You're a big boy," she says with a shrug. "You've got this."

Our time in Montana was over too fast. Next time, we'll stay a minimum of two weeks.

I've already begun looking at some property there. Real estate is like a drug for me. An expensive addiction, yes, but it can also be quite profitable, and if what I've seen so far about the market in Cunningham Falls is true, an investor can't go wrong by buying some property there.

I've just sent off an email to an agent there when my phone rings.

"Hey, Matt."

"This a good time?" he asks, which is code for *are you alone?*

"It is." I sit back in my desk chair and watch the waves beyond the windows of my office. "What's up?"

"There's been some movement," he says. "Mostly in California."

I feel my stomach ease when he doesn't include Oregon.

"You know, it would be easier for me to know what I'm looking for if I knew where in the hell *you* are."

I drag my hand down my face in agitation. I *want* to confide in Matt. But Elena would flip her shit, and I promised her I wouldn't tell a soul.

"I can't," I say at last.

"Archer, I can't protect you like this."

"I'm not asking you to," I reply. "But thanks for having the inclination."

"You're my family, and if you're messed up with this mob family, you could be in serious danger. I can't ignore it."

"I'm not asking you to do that either. Listen, I made a promise that I wouldn't say anything to anyone about this. I've already done too much by calling you in the first place, but I needed the intel."

"I'll continue feeding you information as I get it. Is

there a specific part of the country I should be keeping a close eye on?"

"Matt—"

"You can't tell me. Right." He sighs heavily. "This is fucking frustrating, Archer."

"I know. I don't disagree."

"How long?"

"I don't know that either. Could be weeks. Could be longer."

I don't want to tell him that it could be years. I don't want to admit that even to myself.

"If you need help, at any time, you call me. I can have law enforcement engaged at a moment's notice, anywhere on this globe, Arch. I fucking mean it. Don't hesitate."

"Thank you."

"Don't fucking thank me. This is what family does. We protect each other. Watch your back. I'll be in touch."

I hang up and stand to walk to the windows.

This is what family does. We protect each other. We ask how we can help. We don't fucking whip and brand those we love.

I wish Elena could know what the love of family really means. That she wasn't afraid and running.

But I'm determined to give her that safety.

I just have to figure out *how*.

SEATTLE

17

~CARMINE~

I didn't plan to go back to Seattle emptyhanded. I'd thought to have Elena with me, this whole mystery solved.

I don't like being wrong.

I wait on the plane, ready to go home, as the crew goes through their final checks. Using the family jet is convenient since it's available whenever I want, and I don't have to adhere to the schedules of commercial flights. I'm anxious to get back to Seattle to continue the search for my cousin.

I won't rest until she's home.

"We're ready for you, sir."

I nod at the pilot as my phone rings.

"Don't take off yet. I need to take this call."

"Yes, sir."

He disappears into the cockpit as I answer.

"Give me good news."

"Found him," Shane says into my ear, coming across as pleased with himself. Shane has always been the quiet one, the least emotive, but he sounds downright chipper right now. "He covered his tracks fairly well for a nobody. But I'm no amateur."

"Where is he?"

"Oregon," Shane replies. "Rocco and I are headed there now. I'll text you the exact location and meet you in a few hours."

"Good work," I say as my stomach clenches in anticipation. "Get me that info, and I'll see you soon."

I hang up and buzz the pilot.

"We've had a change of plans."

Three hours later, and my brothers and I are in a booth at a diner in Bandon, Oregon.

"Why don't we just go get her?" Rocco asks.

"Because we don't know for sure that she's with him," I reply. "This could be another wild goose chase. Maybe Archer just happened to buy an investment property here."

"I have a feeling," Shane says, slowly shaking his head. "I feel it in my gut. She's here."

"We need to stake out his house," Rocco says. "We'll see who goes in and comes out."

"Agreed," I reply. "And there's no time like the present. Let's do this."

I throw some bills on the table to cover our coffee, and we file out to the rented SUV parked at the curb.

My adrenaline is up as Rocco follows the GPS to the house on the shoreline. We park down the road so we can still see the driveway but also remain inconspicuous.

"No one's coming in or out without us knowing," Rocco says as he cuts the engine, and we settle in to wait.

Some stakeouts take minutes. Others, days. We have no way of even knowing if Archer's in residence right now.

If all of this is for nothing, I'm going to be royally fucking pissed.

But less than an hour later, a white Audi pulls out of the driveway.

"Let's go."

SEATTLE

18

~ELENA~

"I can't believe you got me a cake." I shake my head at Margie as I bite into my second piece of the chocolate deliciousness. Between this and the donuts I had for breakfast, I'm on a serious sugar high. I really need to give up sugar. I just wish it wasn't so delicious. "You didn't have to do all of this."

"We're happy you're here with us," she says and taps her plastic solo cup to mine before taking a sip of her cola. "Besides, six years as an employee is something to celebrate. As you know, it's not easy to keep loyal employees around here."

"Hey," Chad says with a frown. "I'm only six months behind Ally."

"And you'll get a cake, too," Margie says with a wink. "Thanks for staying a little late so we could celebrate."

"Thanks for the celebration," I reply happily. "It was a nice surprise."

I finish my cake and lean over to hug Margie.

"Also? All those people who quit didn't have the chops for this job. Taking care of baby animals isn't all snuggles and cute photos. It's hard when they die, and when they're sick. It's not a reflection on you, Margie."

"I know. Sucks, though. I sure appreciate you and Chad for stepping up in such a big way over the past year. I don't know what I would have done without you."

"You'd have been on a lot of medication," Chad says with a laugh. "To stop from going crazy."

"You're not wrong."

"Ally's right," Beverly, the new girl, says after setting down a tiny bear cub that was found on someone's back porch. "It's not easy. I know I haven't been here long, but there were moments when I thought I wasn't cut out for this."

"Please don't tell me you're quitting," Margie says, her face transforming into panic.

"No," Beverly says. "I'm not quitting. But the first couple of weeks were rough. So, I also have to give props to Chad and Ally for being here so long."

"I've wanted to do this job since I was a little girl," I admit.

Margie's eyes light up at something behind me,

and I turn to see Archer walking toward me. "I like him."

"Me, too."

He's tanned and wind-blown and everything I've ever wanted in my life. And he's finally mine. He loves me, and he's sticking.

I think it's crazy, and I don't know how we'll work it all out, but I'm here for it.

A woman would be stupid to turn Archer Montgomery down. And I'm no fool.

"You're having a party without me?" Archer asks, his blue eyes intent on the cake, making me laugh. "With food?"

"You'll have to take a piece to go," I inform him. "My car is ready to be picked up. Finally."

"You don't like my car?" Archer's already stuffed one piece of the cake into his mouth and grabbed another for the road.

"I like it fine, but I need my own set of wheels. So, let's go get it."

Margie laughs, waving us off. "See you tomorrow, kiddo."

"Have a good night." We walk out to Archer's Audi. I'm in an *incredible* mood. I feel like I have the best life in the whole world. "They surprised me because I've officially been at the job for six years."

"Very nice," he says and leans over to kiss me. "They're good people."

"Yeah, I think so, too. I'm excited to get my car back. And then I have plans to have drinks with Lindsey later this afternoon after she gets off work. We're just going to the bar at the resort, keeping it simple, but it'll be good to see her. We haven't had any girl time in a long while."

"I love it when you're in a good mood," he says as he kisses my fingers, driving toward the auto shop.

"It's been a wonderful couple of weeks," I say and roll the window down so the breeze can flow through my hair. "I have no complaints."

"I couldn't agree more," he says as he parks in front of the garage. I feel like I'm almost bouncing as we walk inside, and the smell of motor oil and rubber tires hits me.

"Hey, Ally," Lee says with a wave from behind the counter. "We've finally got you all fixed up. Sorry it took so long. We've been pretty swamped."

"No worries. It all worked out." I lean on the counter and smile at the older man. "How much do I owe you?"

He gives me the figure, and I whistle.

"Wow. It was really broken."

"I warned you it would be better to scrap it," Lee says.

"This should get me through for another year." My voice sounds more confident than I feel, and by the look on Lee's face, he also has his doubts.

"I can point you in the direction of an honest used car person when you're ready," Lee says as he passes me my receipt.

"Thanks. For everything. Have a great weekend."

I wave, and with my keys in hand, turn to Archer.

"I'll follow you home?"

"Sounds good, babe." He leans down to kiss me lightly, smacks me playfully on the ass, and we go our separate ways to our vehicles.

Yes, it's a damn good day.

I adjust my seat and mirror, roll down the windows to clear out some of the mustiness from it sitting so long, and start the engine.

It fires up and purrs like a kitten.

Okay, it sputters a bit, but it's running, and that's the most important thing.

Archer pulls out ahead of me, and when I'm behind him, we take off toward his house. I can't help but turn the radio up and sing along with the Journey song wailing through the speakers.

I have a few hours before I'm due to meet with Lindsey. I can either jump on Archer and have my way with him for a while, or head over to my cottage and start cleaning up the remnants of that fiasco.

I just haven't had it in me since the robbery to go in and start dealing with the mess. It's going to take several days. And now that it's been defiled so badly, it's lost its luster for me. I know I'll eventually have to go back and make it my home again, but for now, I'm procrastinating.

Not to mention, I'm in a fantastic mood, and I don't want to ruin it.

So, jumping Archer's bones, it is.

I smirk as I pull in behind Archer in his driveway. Movement in my rearview catches my attention, and I frown when I see a black SUV pull in behind me.

No.

My good mood evaporates, replaced by swift, all-consuming fear.

I step out of my car, just as my cousin Rocco climbs out of the driver's seat of the SUV. But he smiles at me, and that loosens the knot in my stomach, just a smidge.

Then my cousin Shane gets out of the back seat, and when his eyes lock on mine, he winks.

Okay, maybe this won't be so bad.

But then Carmine gets out of the SUV, and the fury on his face has my stomach clenching all over again.

"You have exactly fifteen seconds to get the fuck off my property," Archer says from behind me. He plants his hands on my shoulders, and I watch in horror as Carmine pulls a gun from under his jacket and points it at us.

"Wrong," Carmine says. His jaw is tight, and his brown eyes are locked on mine, his expression filled with hurt and anger and more that I can't read. I want to hug them all. I've missed them. And I'm terrified of what's about to come next. "You're both going to get in the car."

"No," I say immediately and step in front of Archer, shielding him.

"You're coming with us, or I'll kill him here and now. And trust me, Elena, I have no problems doing exactly that."

"He has nothing to do with this," I insist.

"Uh, yeah, babe, I do," Archer says and kisses my hair. "I go where you go."

"No." I turn and stare up into his eyes. "*No.* You can't save me from this."

"I told you," he says, "I'm in for the long haul, no matter how it shakes out. I'm not leaving you to fend for yourself. I'll never do that to you."

"It's too dangerous."

"As entertaining as this lover's spat is," Shane says, "we have things to do. Get in the fucking car. Both of you."

I press my lips together and will myself not to cry. This is it. This is the moment when my life is being torn away from me. The moment when everything I've worked so hard for over the years is just *gone.*

"Hey." I turn at the sound of Rocco's voice. He's standing closer now, and his voice is softer than Carmine's. "We really do need to go, Elena. Once we get where we're going, we can talk, okay?"

"You have to promise me you won't hurt him."

"You know I can't do that," Rocco replies. "Come on. We'll figure this out."

Archer takes my hand in his and leads me to the black SUV.

We have no choice.

I don't know how much time passes. No more than a few hours, I'd guess. We flew in the family's plane to Seattle and are holed up in an apartment in the heart of downtown.

"I thought for sure you'd take us to Uncle Carlo's office," I say to Carmine, who's currently pacing the floor.

"Why would we do that?"

"Because he's the boss."

His eyes narrow into slits. "So you have been paying attention to the family all these years."

"I had to keep tabs on things. I'm not stupid, Carmine."

His hands slide into his pockets, and he doesn't look away from me when he says to the others, "Give Elena and I some time alone."

"You heard the man," Rocco says, nudging Archer out of the room.

"I stay wherever she is," Archer insists.

"He won't hurt me," I say. "He's mad at me, but I'm safe with him, Arch. I promise."

Archer squeezes my shoulder and then leaves the room with my cousins, and Carmine and I are left alone.

God, how I've missed this man. He was basically a brother to me my whole life. He was my protector. My confidante. My best friend.

"What—?" I begin, but he cuts me off with one look.

"What the fuck were you *thinking*?" he demands.

"At what point, Carmine? When my parents were brutally murdered, and I was afraid I was next?"

"We would have protected you," he says, pacing the room again. "*I* would have protected you."

"How? They managed to kill my father, and as much of a bastard as he was, he wasn't stupid. He couldn't protect himself or my mother. I was a sitting duck, and Grandma knew it. So, she got me out of there and told me to wait for her to send for me. Which she never did."

"Un-fucking-believable," he growls and pushes his hand through his dark hair. "Do you realize that we thought you were dead? The three of us *mourned* you."

"I'm sorry." My voice is soft as I think of these three men that I love so much hurting over the thought of losing me. "I'm so sorry that it had to be that way."

"It *didn't* have to be that way. After everything I've been through in my life, I've never felt this betrayed, Elena. And I didn't expect that treachery to come from *you*, someone I trusted with my life."

"It's not like I deliberately did anything to you," I say in my defense. "I had to disappear. And for eight years, I've been safely hidden away, living my life. I will *not* apologize for loving that life, Carmine."

"So, you go away, and you live your fun life away from the family for eight fucking years. None of us knows. And then one day, you attend a funeral, and we find out about it, and we're supposed to just leave you be?"

"So you did recognize me."

"I'd know you anywhere," he says. "Not only did you betray me by leaving, but now I have to punish you, Elena. I have to hurt you, the one person in this world that I *never* want to hurt. All because you couldn't be loyal to the family."

"I DIDN'T CHOOSE THIS FAMILY!" I yell, surprising us both. "I don't want any part of this life, Carmine. And I'm sorry if that hurts your feelings because I love you so much, but the mafia life isn't something I want."

"That's not how this works, and you know it." He paces away and then comes back to me again. "You don't get to fucking choose."

"Now you sound like my father."

"Your father was a pitiful excuse for a human being. He was a horrible boss, and a deplorable husband and father. But in this, he wasn't wrong, Elena. You don't walk away from this family, or from this life. Gram gave you an eight-year vacation, and that's over. It's time to get back to real life and accept the consequences of your actions.

"But I'll tell you this: no matter how much you hate the fact that you're part of this family, you can either make it work for you or against you. That's something you never understood."

"It's always against me if I can't be with the man I love, Carmine."

"That's another thing," he says and shoves his hands into his pockets. "You didn't trust *me* enough to let me know that you were okay, that you were hiding, but you've been shacking up with Archer all this time?"

I shake my head. "You obviously haven't been watching me for long. Archer found *me* about a month ago."

"And you just fell right back into bed with him."

I feel the blood drain out of my face and then surge back into my veins with fury.

"Let me be clear, Carmine. We didn't split up because we fell out of love. We split because my father beat the shit out of me and threatened to kill him if I didn't break it off."

Carmine's eyes turn sober.

"He *hurt you?*"

I turn and lift my shirt and hear Carmine's quick gasp from behind me.

"He tortured me for days, then showed me a live feed of Archer and his sister, with one of his goons ready to fucking kill them both. I wasn't given a choice. Because I don't have the right to choose, remember?"

"You never told me that he did that to you. You *know* that goes against what we believe in."

"And you know that he didn't give a shit about me. He just wanted to control me. In any way he could. So, yeah, when Grandma gave me the option to run away, I grabbed onto it with both hands, and I never looked back. No matter how much I missed you and Shane and Rocco. Because any family who would do *this* to me is one I want no part of."

"Well, you're back now," he says, and then his shoulders sag in defeat. "Fuck, Elena. I'm sorry I couldn't protect you from that piece of shit. I'm sorry that he ever laid hands on you. I would have been there—"

"You were hardly more than a kid yourself, with no clout in the family yet, Carmine. There was nothing you could have done."

I feel the tears threatening.

"I know you're angry and hurt, but I did miss you.

All three of you. And I wondered about you often. When I came home for Grandma's funeral, I wanted nothing more than to hug you. I walked right past you. I knew I shouldn't have gone at all, but I loved her so much. I had to thank her for saving my life."

He turns to look out the window.

"A part of me died when you left," he admits, his voice quiet again. "I think the *good* parts of me died."

"That's not true." He turns back to me with tormented eyes, and I can't hold back any longer. I walk to him and wrap my arms around him, holding on tight. Slowly, he returns the hug, and we stay that way for several long moments. "You're a good man, Carmine."

"No. I'm not, Elena. I can't be given the line of work I'm in. But I love you, and I'll do what I can to protect you."

I pull back to look up into his handsome face.

"What will Uncle Carlo do?"

He sighs. "I don't know."

Seattle

19

~ARCHER~

I'd consider this apartment beautiful if I weren't being held in it against my will. Actually, that's not correct. I'm here willingly because they have the love of my life, and I'll do whatever needs to be done to keep her safe. Leaving her alone with Carmine was like tearing a limb from my body. Everything in me screamed not to let her out of my sight.

But she was so calm about it, so sure that she was safe with the man. Not to mention, I didn't exactly have a choice with Rocco holding a gun to my side.

"So, you're the infamous Archer," Rocco says after leading me into the master suite from the living room, where Carmine is having words with Elena right now.

"And you three are the cousins."

This room doesn't have a bed in it. Instead, it's set up as an office. A large desk fills the middle of the room with several computers, a printer, and more paperwork than I would expect on the surface. Then again, I have no idea how much paperwork it takes to run a mafia family. There's a chair behind the desk, two in front of it, and a small couch off to the side.

It looks like the Martinellis have set this place up as some kind of home base so they don't have to use their private homes or offices for the dirtier jobs.

If I wasn't so fucking pissed, I'd be impressed.

"We should probably tie him up," Rocco says to Shane, but I scoff and shake my head, getting their attention.

"Why?" I hold my hands out at my sides. "We're here willingly. I'm not going anywhere unless it's with Elena. I won't run."

Shane watches me with calm, cool, blue eyes. All three men have an air of danger around them. On a normal day, I would avoid fucking with them.

This isn't a typical day.

"What's he doing to her in there?" I ask, pacing to the door to try to hear anything, and then turning back to them. "No offense, but I don't trust any of you."

"He won't hurt her," Shane says. He stands by the windows, his arms crossed over his chest. All three were wearing suits, but they've since shed their jackets and rolled the sleeves of their white shirts up to their elbows. All of the brothers are tall and broad with dark hair. Carmine's and Rocco's eyes are dark, while Shane's are blue.

"You, on the other hand," Rocco adds, "might want to worry about your own skin."

"What are you going to do to me?" I lean my shoulder against the wall, facing them. "Skin me alive? Shoot me in the knees? Cut off my fingers at the knuckles? Will I be swimming with the fishes?"

"None of that today," Shane says. "But Pop will want to meet you sooner or later, and then it'll get interesting."

My phone, which they confiscated right away and set on the desk in the middle of the room, lights up.

"Your phone's been blowing up all day," Shane says, peering down at the screen. "Who's Lindsey? Are you two-timing my cousin?"

I laugh. "No. That's Elena's best friend. She has my number because Elena doesn't have a cell phone. They were supposed to have drinks today. She's probably wondering where Elena is, and why she's been stood up."

The screen lights up again. If they plan to monitor my phone all day, it'll be a full-time job. It never stops.

"And Matt?"

"My cousin." I see Shane's eyes shift to Rocco. "But you already know that. Your family dug up everything there is to know about mine *years* ago. So, you know who they are. When they can't reach me, they'll start a search, and it won't be a tiny neighborhood watch."

"Oh, look at that," Shane says, his voice as dry as

the desert as he throws my phone on the floor and smashes it with the heel of his boot. "I've just run out of fucks. It doesn't matter to me who your family is. You're dealing with *my* family now, Montgomery."

"You should have just stayed away from her," Rocco says, joining the conversation. "If you'd minded your own business, life would be so much easier for you."

"She *is* my business."

"How long have you been shacked up together? Since she left eight years ago?"

I frown. They obviously don't know as much as they want me to think they do.

"I found her a month ago," I reply. "I was done being without her."

"Maybe it wasn't explained to you the way it should have been," Shane says as he walks away from the window. "It's not just about Elena. It's about the *family*. Her father forbade your relationship because you don't come from the right pedigree. She was supposed to marry someone in another mafia family, to tie the two together and strengthen us as a whole."

"She's a woman, not a business merger."

"She's both," Rocco says. "And she was the only child of the boss. Because she's female, the Watkins name ends with her."

"How are you related?" I ask, truly curious.

"Elena's father and our mother are siblings,"

Shane says. "Our mother married Pop, bringing in the Martinellis to the family. The connection between the Wakinses and the Martinellis goes back generations. Sometimes, it was good. And other times not so good. Our parents' marriage smoothed the relationship, and made the Watkinses stronger than they ever were without us."

"And that was the goal with Elena," Rocco continues. "She was betrothed to a member of the Russian mafia, but that didn't work out for...various reasons."

"What reasons?"

"Those aren't important," Shane replies. "What *is* important is that you understand why you'll never marry Elena, and why you can't be a member of this family. If you're brought in, your loyalties have to change immediately. Family first."

"And he means the mafia family," Rocco clarifies. "Not your family, or Elena. The organization as a whole."

"Your family, the people you care about and come from, will no longer exist in your world. You'll be completely consumed by the Martinellis and their needs."

Bull. Shit.

"I can see that doesn't sit well," Shane says. "And it shouldn't. We're not a normal situation. Unless you're born and bred into it, it seems wrong. But it's not. It's just...different."

"Killing and blackmailing aren't wrong?" I ask.

Rocco cracks his knuckles. "They probably deserved to get dead."

I shake my head and turn back to the door, wondering what's happening in the living room.

"You're not going to talk me out of what I want, gentlemen."

"So, you're willing to risk your family, your business, *everything* for Elena? You'd choose her over those you love the most? Because that's what it boils down to, Archer." Shane tilts his head to the side, watching me carefully. "What are you willing to do? What are you willing to give up for the woman you say you love?"

"God, I'm so tired," Elena says. It's twenty-four hours later, and nothing has changed. We're in the same apartment, wearing the same clothes, stuck with the same people.

The difference there is, the cousins have taken turns sleeping.

We aren't allowed to do that.

"I don't understand this particular form of psychological warfare," I say, keeping my voice mild when I feel anything but. I long to stand and pace the room, punch a wall. *Anything*. "You keep us awake for what?"

"Mental exhaustion is just one way to wear a person down," Elena says with a sigh and leans her head on my shoulder. We're curled up on the couch together while Carmine and Shane work on laptops at the dining room table. "It's an old trick. Guys, just let me nap."

"No," Carmine says as he continues tapping on the keyboard of his laptop.

"What do you want?" I ask, still mindful to keep my voice calm. "Are you wearing us down to talk about something? Do I have information you need? What's the end goal here?"

Carmine looks up from his computer. "We want you to willfully leave Elena be. To agree to disappear from her life forever."

"No."

Elena stiffens beside me. "Are you fucking serious?" she demands. "*That's* what this is about?"

"What did you think it was about?" Shane asks.

"I thought you were just holding us here and being jerks until Uncle Carlo decided to stop by."

"That's only part of it," Carmine says. "The *end goal,* as Archer put it, is for him to leave permanently."

"Not going to happen."

"No?"

"No."

Carmine sits back in his chair and sighs. "I get it,

Archer. Elena's easy to love. She always has been. But don't do this to yourself. You won't win."

Oh, yeah, motherfucker? Try me.

Carmine stands and, with his computer, walks to us, sitting on the arm of the sofa as he taps some keys.

A photo comes up of Rocco squatting next to two little girls at a park, and I feel my blood run cold.

"Who's that?" Elena asks.

"My cousin's daughters."

I'm going to rip your damn eyeballs out of your skull.

"Seems your cousins drop their kids off at birthday parties and just leave." Carmine clicks his tongue. "That's not very safe. Anyone could just walk right up to little Olivia and Stella here and snatch them away. Look at how they're laughing at what Rocco's telling them."

"When was this?" Elena asks.

"This afternoon," Carmine says as if he's talking about what kind of flowers he plans to plant in his garden this year. "Oh, look at this one. It really is fun to look at photos of your family."

He taps the arrow key, and a new picture fills the screen.

"Anastasia, isn't it?" he asks. "She's beautiful."

If you touch a hair on her head, they will never find your fucking body.

"Looks like she's leaving a women's health clinic. Did you know she's pregnant?"

What? I have to fight not to blink quickly or stand and demand to leave so I can call her. Pregnant? That news is amazing and fantastic.

And I'll murder these assholes myself if they touch her.

"Oh, my God," Elena whispers, gripping onto my arm. "Carmine, no."

"It would be a shame, wouldn't it, if Anastasia was in a horrible car accident and they both died?"

You. Mother. Fucker.

But my expression is impassive when he looks down into my face.

"Carmine, this is *insane*. Since when do we threaten the lives of innocent people?"

"Since always," he says, not even sparing her a glance. "You've just been very sheltered, Elena."

"No," she says and stands to pace, stopping by Shane. "Stop this."

"Don't you have anything to say?" Carmine asks me.

"What do you want me to say?"

He shuts the computer with an angry snap and paces away from me. "Don't you give a shit about your family, Archer?"

"You haven't been *listening* to me," I reply as I stand and prop my hands on my hips. "They aren't some small, meek people in the middle of nowhere that you can bully. If you do this, if you hurt anyone I love, you have no idea the wrath they will unleash on you. On all of you. You think the fucking mafia is scary? Try fucking with the Montgomerys. We have deep contacts with law enforcement, with the military. Hell, the O'Callaghans may have ties with the Irish Mafia, for all we know. The connections and money my family has are endless, and they will *end you* if you hurt us."

Shane laughs, surprising Elena. "I have to respect your arrogance, Montgomery. You're foolish, but you're confident."

"Nothing I've said is a lie," I reply.

"Archer," Carmine begins and walks to me, putting his nose only inches from mine. "We know everything there is to know about you and your *connections.* Do I look concerned?"

"You should be."

"No, my friend." He shakes his head. "*You* should be worried. Because that wrath you speak of? It's about to rain down in ways you've never dreamed of."

"I'm not your friend." I stare at him, unblinking. "Bring it."

Less than an hour later, Rocco returns to the apartment with an older man that looks just like him. With his dark hair slicked back, dressed in a dark suit with a dark shirt, and the signature mafioso ring on his right little finger, this man screams *mafia boss*.

I glance down and see Elena shrink against me as if she's a scared little girl afraid of the bogeyman.

And that pisses me right off, igniting more anger in me than I've felt even in the time we've been here. Even after Carmine threatened my family.

"Uncle Carlo," Elena says and lifts her chin, but she doesn't pull away from me.

The man stops in front of us. His face is stern, but his dark eyes soften as he stares at the woman he hasn't seen in many years.

"Little one," he says and immediately tugs Elena into his arms for a firm hug. "Oh, how I've missed you, sweet girl."

In her shock, she doesn't hug him back right away, but then her arms encircle him, and she holds on tightly.

"Are you surprised?" he asks when he finally pushes her away.

"Shocked," she admits.

"Oh, don't get me wrong. We'll be having a stern conversation before the night is out, but for right this minute, I want to look at you. You're a beautiful woman, Elena. And a smart one."

He pats her cheek and then walks away without even acknowledging that I'm standing here.

"Maybe too smart," he continues. "However, you

underestimated me. You see, Elena, I've known where you were since the minute you left Seattle eight years ago."

Elena's eyes grow wide, and Carmine rounds on his father.

"What the fuck are you talking about?" Carmine demands. "You *knew*? Why would you send us off on some wild goose chase if you already knew where she was? I just wasted weeks of my life."

Carlo is impassive as he stares at his eldest son. "Because, my dear boy, you have to earn my trust back."

He dismisses Carmine and turns back to Elena.

"You know there's a price to pay for deserting the family the way you did."

"Grandma sent me away," Elena replies. "For my own safety."

"That wasn't her call to make," he says easily. "She wasn't in a position to make those decisions. Do you think the men she called to help with your arrangements didn't immediately report back to *me*? They were my employees, not hers."

"Then if you knew where I was, why didn't you come for me before now?" Elena asks.

"Because I didn't have a need for you. You were safe, and I kept an eye on you."

She narrows her eyes. "I've seen black SUVs around town, but I always brushed them off."

Carlo smiles. "See? I told you, you're a smart girl. We kept tabs on you, watched out for you. That break-in you had a few weeks ago was unfortunate. I suppose boys will be boys."

"Holy shit," Elena whispers.

"So, yes. I knew you were safe, and I didn't need you, so I left you be. You'd endured enough at the hands of your father, piece of shit that he was."

On that, we could agree.

"So, why now?" Elena asks. "What do you need from me now?"

"Why, nothing. But you came to the funeral. Mistake number one." He strides across the room and sits on a stool by the kitchen island, leaning an elbow on it as he turns to us conversationally. "I knew the minute you left Bandon with your little friend here."

His eyes turn to me.

"And I'll get to you in a moment. I was surprised when I didn't see you in the crowd at the church, but I was busy mourning my mother-in-law and seeing to the service. I would have left things alone and let you return to Bandon and live your life for a while.

"But Carmine recognized you."

Carmine shakes his head and rubs his hand over his mouth in frustration. He's seething. All three brothers look as if they're ready to kill their father themselves.

"So," he continues, "I couldn't very well brush it

off, could I? And, I'll be honest, it didn't sit well with me when I found out that Archer had found you."

He turns to me now, his eyes cool.

"You've been an issue for my family for way too long, Mr. Montgomery."

"Uncle Carlo—"

"But I'll expand on that in a moment. First, there are consequences for what you did, Elena. A price to pay for leaving and for doing so much in your power to stay gone, as if you don't want any part of us at all."

"I don't," she says and crosses her arms over her chest.

"Well, I'm sorry to hear that. Now—"

"I'll take her punishment," Carmine says. "It's my fault that she's here. I'll take it."

Carlo takes a deep breath. "Noble. But no, that's not possible. You know that's not how this works. You have to dole out the punishment, my boy."

"You won't touch her," I say, speaking for the first time since he walked into the room. "*I'll* take her punishment."

"Brave," Carlo says, his eyes brightening as he thinks it over. "And this becomes an all new ballgame.

"No." Elena takes my hand in hers. "Archer, no."

"I accept," Carlo says, watching Elena. "But you won't get off scot-free, little one. No, your punishment is that you have to watch. Every moment. Every single thing that's done, you'll watch, and you won't beg for it to stop."

"Uncle Carlo—"

"It's settled." He motions to his sons. "Clear the room and tie him up, then we'll get started. There's no time like the present."

SEATTLE

20

~ELENA~

No. No no no no no. This is my worst nightmare come to life. I watch in horror as Rocco and Carmine move the furniture to the edges of the room, and then Shane places a kitchen chair in the middle.

"Have a seat," Carmine says, gesturing to the chair.

"No. Please, no." I grab onto Archer's arm, but he turns to me, frames my face in that special way he does, and smiles down at me.

"Hey, it's okay, E. Everything's going to be okay." He kisses me softly and then turns away, sitting in the chair. Before Rocco can even start tying his hands down at his sides, securing them to the legs of the chair, Shane hauls off and punches Archer in the face.

"Jesus," I mutter and crush my fist to my mouth.

"It'll be over before you know it," Uncle Carlo says with a wink. "Now, I won't tie you up unless you do something stupid like run in there and get yourself hurt. Stay on this stool."

I can't move. I *want* to. Everything in me screams to run to him, to cover him with my body so I can absorb the beating and not him.

But if I do, I'll only make things worse for him.

So, I stay put and feel my eyes glaze over as Rocco pulls a bullwhip out of a gym bag.

"No," Carmine says, glancing at me. "Not the whip."

"Why the fuck not?" Rocco asks.

"Show them," Carmine demands. I shake my head no, but he advances on me, spins me around, and pulls up the back of my shirt.

"What the fuck is this?" Uncle Carlo exclaims. "Did this prick do this to you?"

"Of course, not," I growl, turning to my uncle with a glare. "My *father* did it."

He sputters, and his face flushes with fury as I yank my shirt down and turn back around. His jaw tightens, and he merely nods at my cousins.

Rocco tosses the whip aside but pulls a hammer out of the bag instead. Archer's eyes don't leave mine as Rocco rears his arm back and brings the hammer down on Archer's hand, smashing it against the leg of the chair.

"Motherfucker," Archer growls, his body shaking in pain and anger, but he still doesn't look away from me. It's as if he's soaking in *my* strength, my love for him, to use as a shield against what's about to come.

The three of them take turns, punching and kicking him until he's a bloody, swollen mess, breathing hard and sweating profusely.

I glare at all three of my cousins, silently damning them to hell for putting Archer through this insane pain.

But Archer doesn't cry out again. He winces, but he never once begged for the torture to stop. Archer pants hard, his tanned skin streaked with his blood and sweat. His head begins to fall forward in exhaustion.

"Well. Now he's ready," Uncle Carlo says with a smile. "Untie him and let's see what he has left in him. If he fights back and manages to survive the beating, I'll let him live."

"You'll do better than that," Archer says with a growly voice. "You'll let me marry Elena."

Uncle Carlo's face transforms from agreeable to rage in an instant.

"Who do you think you are to tell me what I'll agree to?"

"I'm taking her punishment for leaving eight years ago," Archer continues, not retreating from my uncle in the least. "If I win this fight, you'll give us your blessing to marry. This is more than a decade in the making, Carlo, and you know it. We've earned it."

I'm watching Archer's face as he struggles to

breathe through the pain, blood dripping down his cheek from the side of his swollen eye. His dark hair is wet with sweat, and his naked torso gleams in the light from the setting sun behind him.

"Let's see if you win first," Uncle Carlo sneers and nods at my cousin Shane to untie Archer.

We're surrounded by my family, all of them hell-bent on torturing Archer. On keeping us apart.

But after more than ten years, I'm done being without him.

While the cousins untie him, Archer's gaze never leaves mine.

I love you, he mouths.

I love you, too, I mouth back.

Finally, his hands are free, and he pushes to his feet.

"Rocco," Uncle Carlo says. "Take care of him."

The three gang up on him, but when Carmine and Shane hold his arms so Rocco can punch him, Archer uses the two brothers as leverage to kick up his legs and knock Rocco out.

My cousin falls in a heap on the floor, unconscious.

I feel Uncle Carlo shift next to me, and we watch silently as Shane throws a punch. Archer deflects, captures Shane's hand, and while bending it back until there's a loud *snap*, Archer punches the heel of his injured hand into Shane's nose, sending him falling to the floor, as well.

"Maybe we underestimated you," Carmine says, wiping at the sweat dripping from his forehead.

"In more ways than you realize." Archer's voice is hard and gravelly, filled with determination and grit. Hope fills my belly when Carmine moves to punch Archer, but he deflects. Archer is going to win this! We're going to leave here and be together.

But Carmine rounds on Archer and tags him from behind. He wraps his arm around Archer's neck and holds him in a headlock. Both men grunt from the exertion, their skin red. Archer's face is turning purple. My God, I want to run to him, help him. Carmine could kill him!

"Don't." That's all Uncle Carlo says.

And then I watch in fascination as Carmine leans in and whispers something in Archer's ear.

We can't hear what is said, but the next thing I know, Archer grips the arm around his throat with his good hand and pulls down hard, then flings his head back and connects with Carmine's nose, sending blood spraying everywhere as Carmine falls to the floor.

Archer stands in the middle of the room, chest heaving, eye swollen shut, and covered in blood. But his eyes are on me as he says, "I win."

I wait. I want to beg Uncle Carlo to do the right thing. I *know* that he's a good man deep down. I felt the love he had for me when he wrapped me in his arms.

Uncle Carlo rubs his hand over his chin and watches Archer thoughtfully, ignoring the groans coming from his sons on the floor.

"Carmine was right, we did underestimate you. I'll concede that you won."

"I'm taking Elena, and we're leaving. We're *leaving*. She won't ever see you again."

"I won't agree to that," Uncle Carlo replies. "You know that's not possible. She can never leave. It's been a hard lesson to learn."

He turns his eyes to me.

"I'll allow you to marry, if that's what she wants."

My heart soars. Is this really happening? But then the reality of it hits me right between the eyes.

"I can't." I turn to Archer. "I can't let you get sucked into this. Maybe we can run and hide again."

"We're done running," Archer says and hobbles to me, wrapping his arm around my shoulder. "No more hiding. No more. There's not much I can do for you, Carlo."

"You'd be surprised," my uncle replies with a thin smile. "I'll approve of this match, with the understanding that if and when I need you, I'll call on you, and you'll answer. If you hide from me, we'll find you. And it won't end as well as it did for you today."

"I told you," Archer says, "I'm done hiding. But I have a condition of my own."

My uncle's eyes narrow, but he doesn't say anything as Archer continues.

"You'll leave *my* family alone. They have no part in this, and you'll never hold them over my head again. My family is as important to me as yours is to you, Carlo."

He waits for a heartbeat, and then Uncle Carlo nods once. "Agreed."

Without another word, Archer and I walk to the door. I glance back at my cousins on the floor, but Uncle Carlo is already on the phone, calling in the medical team that he keeps on the payroll to help.

"Where are we going?" I ask once the elevator doors close, and Archer leans heavily on the wall. "My God, you can hardly stand."

"Get me home."

"I'm going to get you to a hospital, that's where I'm taking you."

"No." He shakes his head and then grimaces. "Home. I'll make some calls."

"Archer—"

"For once, just do as you're told, Elena."

I want to yell at him and maybe smack him for having the audacity to speak to me like that, but I can't argue because he just leans his head on mine and sighs.

"I love you, babe. Was worried I might not walk out of there."

"I love you, too."

We're at Archer's house in West Seattle, and he's been in and out of consciousness.

I don't know what to do, so I call Anastasia from Archer's landline.

"I need your help," I say immediately and tell her about Archer's condition. "He won't let me take him to the hospital. I'm worried his hand is broken, and I think he might have a concussion. What am I going to do?"

"Sit tight," she says brusquely. "I'll be there with a doctor in less than thirty minutes."

She hangs up, and I run a washcloth under ice-cold water, then press it to Archer's forehead. He's burning up.

"I called your sister," I say softly. "I'm so worried. Why won't you go to the hospital?"

"Too many questions," he mutters. "I'll heal. Had worse."

"Yeah, right." But he's done what he likely intended and made me smile. "She said she'll be here in a few with a doctor."

"Jase," he says. "Lia's brother-in-law. Surgeon."

"Good." I dab at his wounds with the rag. He needs more attention than I can give him here with no supplies.

He's just drifted off again when the doorbell rings. I sprint downstairs and fling open the door, relieved to see Anastasia and a man holding a medical bag.

"Where is he?"

"In the bedroom."

They both step inside, and Jase takes off up the stairs.

"That's Jase," Anastasia says before pulling me in for a massive hug. "He's a doctor."

"Archer told me." I hug her back, just as fiercely. "Hi."

"Oh my God, it's so good to see you. I was afraid I'd never see you again."

"I know." I pull back and take her in. "Wow. You're not a kid anymore."

"Neither are you." She smiles and we walk to the couch, where we sit and hold each other's hands. "What happened?"

"So much." Everything pours out of me. Archer finding me. Falling back in love with him. Getting caught in Bandon and being hauled back here. Everything that happened over the past two days. "I'm so sorry. He's broken and hurting up there because of *me*. And that's the last thing I ever wanted to happen, Stasia. It's why I broke it off all those years ago because I was afraid of exactly this happening. They could have killed him."

"But they didn't," she says, covering my hand with her own. "And he's strong. Besides, now you can be together without hiding."

"I don't know." I shake my head slowly. "I've been thinking about it since we left the apartment. Uncle Carlo said we could be together, but only if Archer agreed to be a part of the family and do whatever needs to be done when Uncle Carlo needs him. I can't ask that of him. I don't want him to get swept up in my family. I think it's best if I make sure Archer's well, and then I leave again."

Anastasia's eyes are narrowed as she listens, and then she blows out a gusty breath.

"Have you lost your fucking mind?" she demands. "First of all, if you run again, he'll just find you. Or I will and beat the snot out of you. Second of all, if you break my brother's heart again, I'll still beat the snot out of you."

"You've become very violent since I last saw you."

"You mess with my brother, and you bet your ass, sister. You weren't there to pick up the pieces after you broke up with him before. I was. It was horrible. And then when he found out *why* you ended it, and went on a bender, singing songs in my husband's family's bar? Yeah, it wasn't pretty."

"He told me. I wish I'd seen the singing part."

"No, you don't. It was embarrassing as hell. *Then* he was like a man possessed. Whenever he had a spare minute, he was searching for you. He loves you *so much* he risked his life today to be with you. And you're ready to walk away from that? Jesus, Elena, I hate to ask just what your standards are in men if this isn't good enough for you."

"I feel guilty. I feel like I'm asking too much of him."

"Do you think my brother does anything he doesn't want to do? He's as stubborn as they come. And he wants *you*. Any way he can get you. Why don't you hold on to that? Why don't you believe in the love you have with Archer and be grateful for it? Live your life, *Elena*. Not Ally. Live Elena's life, and be happy. Every day. If your family kicks up some drama here and there, you'll deal with it. But living in *what-ifs* and trying to stay ten steps ahead of a possibility that might not ever happen is no way to survive."

I swallow hard and brush at the tears falling on my cheeks.

"You're right."

"Of course, I'm right."

We turn as Jase comes walking down the stairs.

"How is he?"

"Someone beat the shit out of him," Jase says. "I'm Jase, by the way."

"Elena." I shake his hand. "Does he have a concussion?"

"A slight one," he confirms. "You'll want to wake him every two hours and check the dilation of his pupils. I cleaned up the wounds, and the dressings will need to be changed daily. I'd like to have that hand x-rayed. And I think there may be some fractured ribs, as well."

"Jesus," Anastasia says. "How many were there?"

"Three against one," I reply, my voice grim. "Meds?"

"Ibuprofen every four hours as needed. If he needs anything stronger, let me know, and I'll write a script. He needs rest, so don't let him decide to run a marathon this weekend."

I smile. "I won't. Thank you very much."

"Call me if you need anything." Jase passes me his card. "My cell number is on there."

"You can call me, too. And tell my brother to call me tomorrow when he's up to it," Stasia says.

"I will. Thank you both. You didn't have to do this."

"This is what family does," Jase says with a wink.

When they're both gone, and Jase has given me more instructions for ice, rest, and elevation, I check on Archer. He's sound asleep, so I take a quick shower to get the last forty-eight hours off me and find a T-shirt of Archer's to slip into.

When I return to his bedside, he's still sleeping,

breathing slow and steady. It's not time to wake him up yet, so I just slip into bed next to him with my head propped on my elbow and lay on my side to watch him.

I almost lost him tonight. They might have killed him. I don't believe my cousins wanted that, but what they want doesn't always matter.

As I well know.

Archer's legs become restless, and he moans in his sleep. I brush my fingers through his hair, still stained with blood, and murmur to him.

"It's okay, my love. You're okay. No one's going to hurt you."

He opens the one eye that's not swollen and turns to me. "Thought you were a dream."

"No, I'm right here."

"We won," he says before his eye drifts shut again.

"Yes, we did."

"Worth it."

"Babe, can I ask a question?"

He reaches out to take my hand in his good one and brings it to his lips, pressing a kiss to the pads of my fingers.

"Anything."

"When you were fighting, what did Carmine whisper to you?"

His lips twitch, and that eye opens again. *"You'd better win this, motherfucker."*

I blink in surprise. "That's what he said?"

"Yeah. I don't think your cousins are bad people, babe. I think the mafia is fucked-up."

"You're right about that." I want to skootch in and cuddle him, but I'm afraid of hurting him, so I lean over and kiss his cheek. "How do you feel?"

"Like someone hit me with a bus."

"Close enough. I have a confession." I lick my lips, watching this strong man before me. This guy that I love so much. "I almost ran again. Because the thought of you being caught up with my family is almost too much for me to bear."

"I'd find you."

I smile, remembering what Anastasia said. "I know. And I had to remind myself that you were right. We're done hiding. I'm going to live every day, one day at a time, with you. Grateful. Because we've earned our life together, Archer. It's been a long time coming."

"I'm glad you finally figured it out," he says, his voice more slurred. "So tired. Gonna sleep, okay?"

"Sleep. We have all the time in the world to be philosophical."

"'kay."

His breathing evens out, and I know he's sleeping once more.

SEATTLE

21

~CARMINE~

I'm sitting in the screened-in porch of my home, waiting for my brothers to arrive. It's a rainy day in the Pacific Northwest, mirroring my mood perfectly. In the week since we found Elena and all three of us took a beating from Archer, I've been planning.

Calculating.

I'm almost ready to set my scheme into motion, but I want to run my thoughts by Shane and Rocco. I'll need their help if this idea is going to be a success.

"Hello?" Shane calls from inside the house.

"Out here," I call back. I'm in gym shorts and a sweatshirt. No shoes. My third cup of coffee sits on the table next to me.

It's barely eight in the morning.

"It's fucking early," Rocco mutters as he walks out

onto the porch with Shane, both holding steaming mugs of coffee from my kitchen.

"Help yourselves."

"We did," Shane says and sits opposite me. Rocco stands with his shoulder against the railing and sips his brew.

Both of my brothers have black eyes, faded from purple to a sickly green now.

I know my face doesn't look any better.

"He really fucked you guys up," I mention casually and cross an ankle over the opposite knee.

"Looked in a mirror today?" Rocco asks.

"He gave as good as he got," Shane adds. "It doesn't feel good, but I have to respect that. He'll protect Elena."

I nod in agreement. "Which leads me to why I asked you to come over here. I've been thinking."

"Whenever you start thinking, I get my ass kicked," Rocco mutters, glowering into his half-empty mug.

I ignore him.

"We've known for a while now who is responsible for Uncle Vinnie's death. It's time we did something about that."

"Why now?" Shane asks.

"A few reasons. Elena's home, so it's time to close that circle completely. Avenging her parents' deaths will do that."

"And?" Rocco asks.

This is the sticky part for me. The bit that leaves a sour taste in my mouth.

"I have to earn Pop's trust, remember?"

Shane's eyes narrow. "Pop was being a dick when he said that."

"He knew where Elena was, and he lied about it and then sent us all on a wild goose chase. It fucking pisses me off. I'm too old to play these games with him. So, I'm going to settle the score all around."

"How?" Rocco asks.

I reach for a photo lying next to my coffee mug, flip it over, and toss it back on the table. Both of my brothers lean in to get a look at the tall, willowy blonde in the picture. She's wearing sunglasses and a short skirt. Her hair is long and straight, and her lips are painted a bold red.

"Nadia Tarenkov" Shane asks with a raised eyebrow. "You're going to infiltrate the Tarenkov family through the boss's daughter?"

"Balls of fucking steel," Rocco mutters as a slow smile spreads over my face.

"What's the saying about revenge?"

"*Revenge is but a small circle?*" Shane asks.

"*Dead men tell no tales,*" Rocco adds.

I laugh and shake my head, lifting the photo of Nadia and studying it.

"I was thinking more along the lines of *paybacks*

are a bitch."

SEATTLE

22

~ELENA~

"Your breakfast, my lady." Archer steps onto the deck at his beach house in Bandon, his arms laden with pancakes and all the fixings. Including bacon. I think the man keeps the pork industry in business all on his own.

"You didn't have to make breakfast," I say as I accept the plate and set it on the arm of the chair next to me, already salivating at the smell of the deliciousness before me. "But I'm grateful."

"We worked up an appetite last night," he says with a wink and takes a huge bite of his pancakes. "We need the calories."

I watch him as I eat, relieved to see that the bruises have faded away. Unless you look closely, you'd never know that he'd been beaten so badly just two weeks ago. Archer kept his word, he healed from the injuries quickly. I had to order, bribe, and beg him to stay in bed longer than two days so he'd heal faster, though.

"I missed it here," I say as I take a deep breath and enjoy the salty air. The water's a little choppy this morning, and birds fly over the waves in search of their breakfast. "We got lucky with the weather this weekend."

"I watched the weather app last week, and it looked like a few storms blew through Bandon. They got it worse here than in Seattle."

I nod and chew my bacon. "I'm going to really miss living here."

He frowns at me. "We own property here."

"Speaking of which, I need to get my cottage cleaned up and ready to put on the market."

"Are you sure you want to do that? You could rent it out. You don't have to sell it."

"I don't know how often I'll be in town, and I don't want to hassle with a rental company. Plus, since it got ransacked, it just doesn't feel like home anymore. It's time to sell and turn the page on that chapter. Are you going to keep this place?"

He swallows and turns to me fully now. "Elena, are you under the impression that we'll go back to Seattle and never come back here?"

I frown, hating the idea of never returning to Bandon. "With your work in Seattle, I just assumed we'd be there most of the time."

"You know I run my own company," he says. "I work just fine from here, and I can do that from time to time. I have no intention of selling this house. I love it here. But most importantly, *you* love it here. So, we'll come whenever you want."

The love is swift and all-consuming, filling me so full, it feels like light will start shooting out of my fingertips any second.

"You're awfully good to me," I say. "I'd like that. I have a busy day ahead. In addition to starting on the cottage, I have to go to the animal refuge and see Margie and Chad. And I'm having drinks with Lindsey this afternoon."

"You finally get your happy-hour time," he says with a grin.

"Yeah. I know they've all been worried and confused. It's time I come clean about everything. I'll miss that job."

"There are animal rescues in and around Seattle," he says. "I'm sure one of them would be happy to welcome you on staff. And like I said, we'll be back to visit. You're not saying goodbye forever like you did in California."

"You're right. I guess it's just an old habit. It's amazing, isn't it? How much can change in six weeks? My life is completely different. For the better."

"Same here," he says. "I'm relieved it's over. That

you've come to an understanding with your family, and we can get on with our lives. It's past time."

"It's because of you that it happened," I reply. "I owe you so much."

"You don't owe me anything, Elena. I'd do anything to keep you safe and make sure you're happy."

"These pancakes are a good start." I grin and don't react when the phone buzzing starts.

"That's yours, babe."

"Oh, right."

When Archer replaced his phone, he got me one, as well. It's the first cell I've owned in almost ten years, and I'm not used to listening for it.

I scowl at the name on the screen.

"Hello?"

"Good morning," Uncle Carlo says. "How are you today, little one?"

"I'm fine." The food I just ate sits like lead in my stomach. "What's up?"

"I need to see you in my office as soon as possible."

I close my eyes and feel despair creep through me. "Already? Uncle Carlo, we just arrived back in Bandon, and we're seeing to a few things here. You need us for something so soon?"

"No, you misunderstand," he says. "I'm not calling you because I need something from you or Archer. I need to see you because we need to discuss your parents' estate. It's been sitting for eight years. And added to that is your inheritance from your grandmother."

"Oh." I blink and look over at Archer, who watches intently. "Honestly, I don't want anything from my parents. I don't care what you do with it."

"I can't do anything with it."

I laugh at that. "Of course, you can."

Uncle Carlo chuckles with me. "Elena, I know you didn't have a close relationship with your parents. But this all belongs to *you*. Real estate, investments, money, jewelry. The value is in the eight figures."

My mouth goes dry, and my tongue sticks to the roof of my mouth as I stare at Archer in shock. I had no idea my parents were worth so much.

"Elena?"

"I'm here."

"You were their only child, and everything was left to you in their will. It's gone through probate, and as the executor, I've been managing it. But it's time for you to take it all over. Now, I honestly don't care what you decide to do with it all, but don't be foolish and turn it down just because your parents failed you. Make it work for you. And if you need advice, I'm always happy to help. But you're a smart woman, Elena."

"Let me do some thinking. I'll be sure to call you

when we're back in Seattle. It'll probably be a week or two."

"That's perfect. Travel safe."

He hangs up, and I open and close my mouth like a fish out of water.

"He said—"

"I heard," Archer says. "You're an incredibly wealthy woman, Elena."

My shoulders sag. "I already was, actually. But this is…unexpected. I guess it never occurred to me to think about what happened with their estate after they died. I left less than forty-eight hours after their deaths and figured anything they had would have been absorbed by the family."

"You assumed wrong," Archer says and reaches over to take my hand. "But don't worry. I'm not just after you because I'm hot for your money."

I chuckle and then start to laugh, the kind of laugh that grabs hold of you, where you're helpless to stop it.

When I finally take a deep breath, tears are running down my face. My stomach muscles ache. My face is frozen in a most unattractive expression, I'm sure. But I don't care. That felt damn good.

"Ally!" Lindsey rushes to me across the lobby of the resort and pulls me in for a tight hug. "I don't know what the hell's been going on, but you've got some 'splaining to do."

"I know." I hug her and then step back. "But first thing's first. My name isn't Ally. It's Elena."

Lindsey frowns and then takes my hand and leads me toward the bar. "I think we need drinks before you say any more."

"Good idea."

We choose a booth in the corner where we'll have some privacy, and once our martinis are sitting in front of us, Lindsey takes a breath.

"Okay. Start from the beginning."

And so, I do. It feels amazing to finally be able to tell my best friend everything, from being with Archer in high school to our separation, then about my parents' deaths, and everything that happened after.

"How didn't I recognize you?" she wonders as she takes the last sip of her drink. "I used to *love* watching the gossip on your family."

"I was never in the spotlight much. I'm an introvert by nature, and I always stayed out of trouble."

"Well, it makes sense."

"What does?"

"That day at the diner when your grandmother's death was on the news, and you flew out of there like a bat out of hell. And Archer—who I like, by the way. He's nice, and he's *hot*."

"I know." I grin, enjoying being with my friend again. "I'm sorry I had to lie to you for so long."

"I'm just sorry that you had to at all. But I'm so glad that it's over for you. Have you already talked to your job?"

"Yeah, I was just there. Margie cried." I feel my eyes fill with tears at the mention of it. "She'd been worried, and she's sad that I have to quit. Archer and I will live in Seattle full-time, but we're keeping his house here. So, you're not getting rid of me. I'll be back to visit and check in on you."

"Damn straight, I'm not losing you," she says. "I'll come visit up there, too. I love the city and don't get to shop nearly often enough. I have a ton of vacation time coming."

"We can meet up in Portland sometimes, too," I suggest.

"Absolutely." She signals to the bartender that we want two more drinks. "What are you going to do with your house?"

"Sell it."

Her eyes get big. "Really? Would you be willing to sell it to me?"

I tilt my head to the side. "I didn't know you were looking to buy a house."

"I wasn't, but I *love* your place. It's so cute and close enough to the water that you can walk to the beach, but not *too* close to make it worth millions." She grins happily and then deflates. "Wait. Unless you are planning to sell it for millions."

"No." I nod at the bartender when he delivers our drinks. He doesn't even look my way. He only has eyes for Lindsey. But she doesn't spare him a glance. When he walks away and is out of earshot, I pounce. "What's going on there?"

"What? Nothing. I don't know what you mean."

She sips her drink, trying to be nonchalant.

"Bullshit. Spill it."

"There's nothing to spill."

I sit back in the booth and cross my arms over my chest, giving her the *liar, liar, pants on fire* look.

"Okay." She leans in and holds her hand up to the side of her face in case he can hear us from fifty feet away. "I slept with him last weekend. I was lonely and feeling a little needy and totally did him. And now, *he's* the needy one."

I press my lips together, trying not to laugh. "He's pretty hot. Was the sex bad?"

"No, it was good."

"Then why are you ignoring him?"

"Because he failed to mention to me until *after* I'd had my third orgasm that he's *married*."

I gasp and glare at the douche canoe behind the bar. He glances our way, and I flip him off.

"*Ally!*"

"Elena," I reply. "And I'm not sorry. Cheating asshole."

"I already sent an email to his wife just before I met with you today. So, his home life is about to *really* suck."

"He deserves it. I hope she chops off his balls. What a jerk."

"Oh, he's totally a jerk. He didn't understand why I was so pissed-off. He said the relationship sucks, and they're probably going to get divorced anyway, so what did it matter? I did manage to slam his fingers in the door when I left, and he tried to run after me."

"Attagirl." I clink my glass to hers.

"Okay, I have a question," she says, already changing the subject. "Like I said before, your family has always been interesting to me. But what's Rocco like? He's always so stern and mysterious in photos."

I swallow quickly before I blow vodka out of my nostrils. "*Rocco?*"

"Yeah. He's totally hot. Come on, help a girl out."

"No." I shake my head vigorously. "Just, no. Absolutely not."

"You're no fun," she says. "But maybe I'll meet him someday."

"Maybe you'll stay away from him," I say, all-business now. "I'm telling you, Lindsey, my family isn't one you want to get all tangled up in."

"I mean, getting tangled with him sounds kind of fun."

"You're incorrigible."

"I do try."

The sun is just starting to set when I pull into the driveway of the beach house. I'm exhausted. Between the manual labor of cleaning my cottage and the emotional strain of seeing my coworkers and Lindsey, it's been a hell of a day.

I'd love nothing more than to get in the hot tub with Archer for a long soak, watch some trashy TV, and then maybe go to bed early.

Yep, it's a wild Friday night for me.

I park in the garage next to Archer's Audi and walk through the mudroom to the kitchen. It occurs to me that I spent all morning at the cottage and didn't feel a connection to the place at all. And I lived there for six years. Yet as I walk into this beach house, it feels like home. I'd like to think it's because of the man waiting for me here. Home is wherever Archer is.

There are a dozen red roses in a gorgeous blue vase on the counter with a note.

E-

I'm down on the beach. Join me. Grab a sweater, it's getting cold.

-A

I guess the soak will come later. I can't resist a sunset stroll on the beach with the hottest man alive.

I smile when I see one of Archer's sweatshirts lying by the sliding glass door. I throw it on and walk down the steps to the sand below.

When I catch sight of Archer and the scene before him, I stop short.

I <3 U has been drawn in the sand, but the heart is made out of lit candles in hurricane glasses. My heart soars because as cheesy as it is, it's exactly like a night twelve years ago in Seattle.

Which tells me he's about to ask me a very important question.

"It's déjà vu, right?" Archer asks as I approach. He stands in the middle of the candle heart, wearing cargo shorts, a green T-shirt, and the biggest smile ever. He holds out a hand for me, and I take it, joining him.

"It was cheesy back then," I say with a laugh. "And it's a little cheesy now. But maybe the sweetest thing I've ever seen."

His incredible blue eyes turn sober as, with his gaze pinned to mine, he lowers himself to one knee and pulls out a gorgeous ring from his pocket.

"The first time I did this, I thought my love for you couldn't be stronger. That I'd never love you more than I did in that moment. But I was wrong,

Elena. I love you more now than ever before, and you're still the woman I want to spend the rest of my life with. I don't want to miss out on one more day with you. I want to grow old with you, have babies and grandchildren, and give you everything you could ever need or want. I tried to live without you, but I was just a shell of myself without you by my side. So, I'm asking you, right here and now, to make me the happiest man in the world and be my wife. Marry me."

I sink to my knees in the sand in front of him and frame his face with my hands.

"I never stopped loving you, Archer. I know, deep in my heart, that we were always meant to be together. It would be my honor to be your wife."

I can't look away from him as he slips the ring onto my finger and then slides his hands into my hair as he kisses me like never before. As if his life depends on it.

He stands and pulls me to my feet and then slings me over his shoulder, carrying me up to the house.

"Hey!"

He slaps my ass, making me bark out a laugh.

"I can walk," I remind him, but take a moment to admire the ring on my finger. The round stone is massive and set classically. It'll be beautiful with any style of wedding band.

"Not fast enough," he says as he runs, with me still on his shoulder, up the steps to the house. He doesn't pause until we're in the bedroom, and he dumps me on the bed.

"Well, that was romantic."

He laughs and joins me, covering me with his strong form. "I suddenly had the urge to have you in my bed. Naked. Writhing. Unable to control yourself."

"Romantic *and* humble? I hit the jackpot."

He kisses me again, and his hands are swift and sure as they strip me bare. He really is talented at unfastening a bra with one hand.

His lips clamp over a nipple as I open for him, hitching my legs around his hips in invitation.

But he doesn't slide home. No, he takes his time, tickling me with his fingers, making sure I'm slick and ready. And only when I *am* writhing beneath him does he bury himself, balls-deep, as he lovingly cradles my head in his hands.

"I've loved you my whole life," he says. "And I can't wait to finally build a life with you."

I gasp as he presses the root of his cock against my clit. I tighten around him, making him swear under his breath. My hands clench his ass, holding him to me tightly. We're as entangled, emotionally and physically, as we've ever been. It's intoxicating. Addicting. And I don't have to give him up, now or ever.

"It's about damn time."

SEATTLE

EPILOGUE
TWO MONTHS LATER

~Archer~

"So, you're getting hitched." My cousin Matt, along with Luke Williams and Shawn O'Callaghan, stand with me at the O'Callaghan Museum of Glass, all holding pints of Guinness as we watch some of the ladies dancing to the music the DJ plays for us.

Anastasia and Kane insisted on hosting our engagement party here at the museum. Elena was hesitant because having a party like this meant we'd be obligated to invite her family, but the Martinellis seem to be having a good time, mingling with the Montgomerys. Despite several members of my family being part of law enforcement.

I know Carlo and the cousins won't try anything shady on a night meant to celebrate Elena. They love her too much for that.

And Carlo and I have had several private conversations, and he's assured me that he respects me too much to go against his word of not doing my family harm.

As shady as Carlo can be, I trust that he'll keep his promise.

"He can't keep his eyes off her," Shawn says. "I'd say it's a damn good thing he's marrying her."

"She's the best thing in the world," I confirm. Luke grins as he watches his wife, Natalie, dancing.

"I understand completely," he says. A woman walking nearby catches his eye, and he motions for her to join us. "This is perfect timing. Shawn, I'd like to introduce you to N—"

"Lexi Perry," the woman interrupts, shaking her head slightly at Luke and giving Shawn her attention. Shawn's eyes light up at the sight of the beautiful redhead.

"I asked Ms. Perry to come to town on business, and thought it was rude of me to leave her alone in the city this evening," Luke continues. "So, I invited her here. After checking with our hosts, of course."

"It's a pleasure to meet you," I say with a nod. "Welcome."

"Congratulations," she replies and shakes my

hand. "I was hesitant to crash the party, but Natalie and Luke assured me it would be okay. And I have to say, your family is incredibly welcoming."

"We always have room for more," I reply. "What do you do, Lexi?"

"I'm a writer."

I feel Shawn stiffen beside me. "Oh? Shawn's also a writer. What do you write?"

"Novels," she says and turns to Shawn, but he holds up a hand, stopping her.

"I'm not here to entertain any new projects tonight," he says.

Lexi's face goes from friendly to cold in a heartbeat. Luke sighs. I can feel in my gut that something just went very wrong.

"That's convenient," Lexi replies. "I'm not here to pitch a project to you, Mr. O'Callaghan. I know who you are, but it's not terribly important to me. I do fine all on my own. Have a good night, gentlemen."

She nods and walks away in her tight black cocktail dress and mile-high shoes.

"So, that was Nora Perry," Luke says, sipping his drink. Shawn's face whips around to stare at Luke.

"She said her name was Lexi."

"Nora is her pen name," Luke says and slaps Shawn on the shoulder. "You just managed to insult the woman you'll be working with starting on Monday." Luke turns to me. "Congratulations again,

Archer. Elena is beautiful and lovely, and we can't wait for the wedding. Now, if you'll excuse me."

He walks away, leaving Matt and I with a stunned Shawn.

"So, you're gonna be working with her, huh?" Matt asks.

"Buggering hell," Shawn growls, the Irish accent kicking up with agitation as he stomps off in the direction Lexi headed.

Matt and I laugh as we watch him leave, and then he takes a sip of his beer.

"I've been pretty pissed at you, man," he says.

"Why's that?"

"Jase told me how beat up you were when he came to clean you up. You should have fucking called me."

"They broke my phone," I say. Our eyes scan the crowd as we talk. "And you and I both know I had to handle that myself. I needed to end it once and for all."

"Could have died."

"I didn't."

But, God, it felt like I might have when I was in the thick of it.

"I don't like that their family is going to be tied to ours."

"I've already handled that, as well."

He watches me for a long moment. "I'll still keep my eyes open."

"I'd expect nothing less."

"Is she worth it?"

"And more." I tap my glass to his. "She's worth everything."

The End

If you're interested in learning more about the Martinelli family, the With Me In Seattle MAFIA is coming in 2021, beginning with Carmine and Nadia's story, *Underboss*. And I have a sneak peek, just for you! Keep reading...

SNEAK PEEK

Here is a look at the next story in the With Me In Seattle series, Dream With Me:

Chapter One

Anastasia

"This isn't going to work."

I blow out a breath and stare at the shit-tastic mess I've scribbled on my sketchpad in disgust.

The idiots who hired me, and no, I don't always refer to my clients as idiots, didn't give me a place to start. When a couple wants a wedding cake, they usually come to me with photos they've pinned on Pinterest or found in magazines. They have colors and flowers they prefer.

They have a bloody vision.

But the people who marched into my bakery a month ago? They had none of that.

"We want you to go with your own vision," they said with wide-eyed smiles and imaginary cartoon hearts bursting over their heads. *"You're an artist, and we wouldn't dream of intruding on your process."*

I appreciate their vote of confidence. I really do. And, sometimes, clients are *too* stringent in what they want.

"I want exactly *this,"* some brides will say, and I have to gently remind them that I don't copy others' work.

But at least tell me what colors your flowers are. Throw me a damn bone!

It's not *my* wedding.

I've been in the wedding cake biz for a dozen years, and while living in California, I was lucky enough to be on *Best Bites TV*, designing and executing massive works of sugar that would make the most discerning art critics weep with joy.

But now I live near my hometown of Seattle, Washington, where my family is, and I've opened a new business here. I love it. It fuels me and exhausts me, just as a person's passion should.

But today, there's nothing in my well of ideas. My muse has decided to go on vacation, and she didn't give me any warning.

Fucking muse.

When this happens, which isn't often, I find it's best to step away from my kitchen.

So, I pack up my sketchbook and pencils, get in the car, and get ready to battle Seattle traffic.

Once on the road, I call my sister, Amelia. She likes to go to museums with me, and sometimes, the conversation alone will get my mind churning with new ideas.

"Hello, favorite sister," she says when she answers.

"I'm headed over to the glass museum," I say immediately. "Wanna go?"

"I would *love* to, but I'm recording today, and I have to do three videos to catch up. I'm sorry."

Lia is a super successful YouTube sensation. She films makeup tutorials and reviews products. With more than three million followers and her own makeup brand in the works, I couldn't be prouder of her.

Not to mention, she has a new husband who keeps her more than busy.

"I get it. I miss you, though. I haven't seen you in weeks. So, let's try to do a girls' night out, okay?"

"Yes, please. I'm down for that."

"Soon. Like, tomorrow night."

"Hold please." She pulls the phone away from her mouth but doesn't bother to cover it, so I can hear everything. "Wyatt? Babe, Stasia's on the phone and wants to do girls' night tomorrow night. Do we have plans? Oh, right."

I tap my fingers on the steering wheel, surprised that traffic through downtown is as light as it is.

"Hey, sorry, I can't tomorrow night. We're supposed to go to a gala for the new cardiothoracic wing at the hospital. Jace asked us weeks ago."

Our family is big and a little confusing. A diagram and a Ph.D. in astrophysics might be necessary to figure out who belongs to whom, and how we all fit together.

Wyatt is Amelia's husband. His brother, Jace, is the chief of staff in cardiothoracic surgery at Seattle General. Jace is a big deal. Actually, there's a lot of that in our family.

"We'll find a night to get together," I reply.

"Actually, you should come with us," Lia says, excitement in her voice. "I have dresses you can choose from and borrow, and I'll totally do your hair and makeup. It'll be fun. Say yes. Say it right now."

"Like my ass will fit in any of your dresses. Besides, I have *so much* work, Lia. I can't waste a whole day on a gala where I won't know anyone."

"You'll know me and Wyatt. And Jace and Joy. Levi and Starla will be there, too."

I sigh because, deep down, I want to go. I don't get to dress up often, and I love hanging out with Wyatt's brothers and their wives. Not to mention, I never get to see my sister.

But I have a wedding cake due on Saturday morning that's only half-decorated, and I really have to get this other cake designed so I can get to work on it first thing on Sunday.

"You're too quiet. You're thinking of a way you can ditch work so you can go, so just *do it*."

I bite my lip. If I stay up all night tonight finishing Saturday's cake, I can make it work.

"Okay. I'll go."

"Yay," Lia says with a little squeak, making me laugh. "Be at my house by noon so we can start getting ready."

"What time is the gala?"

"Eight," she says.

"It will not take eight hours to get ready."

"You're going to look like a goddess when I'm through with you," Lia promises. "See you tomorrow!"

She hangs up, and I wrinkle my nose. The guilt of taking time away from work that I don't have settles between my shoulder blades.

But one of the things I've been working on this year is taking more time for *me*. I moved out of California because it was killing me. I was working fifteen-hour days, seven days a week, and the result of that was illness and despair. I've battled asthma all my life, and the long hours and some of the spices in the bakery were hell on me. Now, I have my own shop where I can control the environment, along with how many hours a day I work, and I can admit, my asthma has been better. Taking care of myself is important.

And taking one day to be with my family is part of that self-care.

Working through the night is totally worth it.

This was the right call. Being out of the bakery today and immersed in art is exactly what I needed for a fresh perspective. Soaking in someone else's vision always renews my passion for my own creativity.

It seems my muse likes to hang out in museums.

And the O'Callaghan Museum of Glass in Seattle is my very favorite of all of them.

I'm sitting on a bench in the middle of one of the exhibit rooms, soaking it all in.

I've never met Kane O'Callaghan, the artist who creates such beauty. He seems to love color, as it's splashed around me. In this room, the glass is shaped like water, waves crashing on beaches with marine life floating around. Blues, greens, and white with splashes of yellow and red here and there tickle my senses.

I can practically hear the beach around me.

With the hair standing on my skin, I reach for my

sketchpad and pencils. With my legs crossed, I get to work, my pad in my lap.

People walk past me, but I hardly notice them. I'm consumed by the design that's taking shape in my head and on the paper. I take breaks, looking up at the glass, the color, the fluidity of the work, and then keep sketching.

I don't know if I've ever drawn a full concept so quickly.

Once I'm finished, I take a deep breath and notice my chest is beginning to feel heavy. I glance around, surprised to see a man sitting on the bench opposite mine, watching me with lazy, green eyes.

"Can I help you?" I ask the handsome stranger. He has dark hair with matching stubble on his chin, and eyelashes framing those bright green orbs.

"I was just going to ask you the same question," he says with a voice laced with milk chocolate.

"I'm just enjoying the exhibit," I say, giving him a polite smile.

"Looks like you're enjoying your little drawing there," he replies, nodding at the pad in my lap. I close it and drop the smile.

"Just working," I say.

"In a museum?"

I blow out a breath of impatience. "Do you work here?"

He tilts his head to the side, watching me. "Not really."

"Then it's none of your business, is it?"

"Are you one of those people who sits in museums and copies the art there because you can't come up with original work of your own?"

"Are you always an asshole, or just today?" I retort, getting more pissed by the second. "Surely, I'm not the only person in the world who gets inspired by art. In fact, I think that's the point of it."

He doesn't say anything, just blinks and watches me quietly. He's not creepy. I don't get a dangerous vibe from him. If I did, I'd run out of here and alert security.

"Can I see the sketch?" he asks, surprising me.

"It's just a—"

"I'd still like to see it." His lips tip up in a half-smile that would melt far stronger women than I, and he holds his hand out, waiting for me to pass over my pad.

Finally, I flip through the pages to what I was just working on and pass it over to the handsome stranger.

His eyes narrow as he examines the crude drawing. I instantly wish I'd used more color and been more thorough, but it's only supposed to be for *my* eyes. A guideline for when I start decorating the cake in just a couple of days.

"There is no water here," he says in surprise and

looks up at me. "It doesn't look anything like the glass in this room."

"Why would it?" I frown. "I'm *inspired*, not copying. Besides, that's just a sketch. When I make the final piece, I'll know what I was thinking when I thought it up."

"I see." He passes it back to me. "I like it very much. You've a good eye."

Is that a slight accent I hear in his voice? I take a deep breath, relieved that the heaviness is gone from my lungs. If I'm not mistaken, I can *smell* him. It's a lovely, woodsy scent that's light and masculine and, well...sexy.

"What are you doing here?" I ask.

He shrugs a shoulder and glances around the room. "Remembering, I suppose."

Before I can ask him what he means by that, a woman comes rushing into the room, her heels clicking on the hardwood floor.

"Kane, we need you in the storeroom. Now, when you see what happened, don't kill anyone."

"If a piece is broken, I can't guarantee that I won't commit murder." He glances back at me. "I guess our pleasant visit is over, then."

"Wait. Are you Kane O'Callaghan?"

"One and the same." He stands and holds out his hand to shake mine. "And you are?"

"Embarrassed," I mutter as I slide my hand into

his. "I won't tell you I love your work. I guess that's clear enough."

"But an artist never tires of hearing it," he replies with a wink before nodding at the frazzled woman. "Have a good time. And take all the time you need."

With that, he hurries away, and I'm left in the amazing room, flustered.

I just met Kane O'Callaghan. I showed him my sketch. He was a bit gruff, borderline rude, and I managed to call him an asshole.

"Good one, Anastasia."

"This is fun," I mutter while Amelia tickles my cheekbone with a fluffy brush. "We don't do this often enough anymore."

"I know. And I get to do this for a *living*. You should be in one of my videos." Her blue eyes widen in excitement. "Seriously, I could do your makeup in the video and show different techniques for working on someone else. It's *so* different from applying my own makeup. It would be fun."

"Maybe one day."

Where Amelia is gorgeous with amazing cheekbones and a slender body, I'm different. We share the same blond hair and signature Montgomery blue eyes, but I'm curvier than she is, with wider hips and boobs.

I'm not exactly the kind of girl who models on fashion vlogs.

Don't get me wrong, I'm fine with how I look. I *like* my curves. And when I'm done up, well, I look pretty fly, but I'm no fashion model.

"We'll do it next month when the new eyeshadow palette releases," she says as if it's all settled. I just stay quiet. I'll do it for her. It seems I'll do just about anything for my siblings.

"Have you talked to Archer lately?" I ask her. Archer is the eldest, and our only brother.

"Yeah, I tried to get him to come with us tonight, but getting our brother in a suit is like talking a fish out of the water."

I laugh at the thought. "It's too bad because he's handsome when he's all dressed up."

"I'm just happy that I managed to get him in a suit for our wedding," Lia replies and stands back to check out her handiwork. "I think you're ready. Next up is the dress."

"Let me see."

"Not until you're dressed." She leads me through her massive master bedroom to the equally enormous closet. "I've chosen three that will look *so* amazing on you."

"I'll never fit into them," I remind her.

"They're A-line, and they'll show off your incredible legs," she says, waving me off. "Try the red one first."

I slip out of the silky robe she insisted I put on so I didn't have to pull a shirt over my head after my makeup was done, and pull the dress up my legs. It gets stuck on my thighs.

"Told you."

"Okay, this one." She passes me a black dress with sparkly fake diamonds scattered across the bodice. Once I wrangle it up over my hips, and she zips up the back, it fits me like a glove. I stare in the mirror, my hands smoothing down the light material. Amelia did a hell of a job on my makeup. But then again, she always does.

"My boobs look fantastic in this," I mutter, admiring the ample cleavage the dress shows off without making me look like I'm a stuffed sausage. The hemline ends just below my knees, and the material floats around my legs like a cloud. "Oh, and it's light and comfy."

"Perfect," Lia says with a bright smile. "It looks ah-mazing on you. You can totally keep it."

"You don't have to—"

"It's Versace."

"I'm totally keeping it."

Lia laughs and steps into her own pink dress that slips off her shoulders, making her look like a faerie princess. Once dressed, she stands next to me, and we admire ourselves in the mirror.

"We're hot, sweet sister of mine," she says. She leans in to kiss my cheek, but I pull away. Lia's always trying to cuddle me, kiss me, or hug me.

I secretly like it, but I can't tell her that.

"Hell, yes, we're hot."

Wyatt's waiting downstairs for us, dressed in a classic black tuxedo, and as soon as we reach him, we're off, headed for the gala. At this time of night, traffic is light, so we quickly reach the hotel where the shindig is being held.

We're helped out of the car, and once inside, I reach for a glass of champagne and look for our people.

"There's our table," Wyatt says, pointing to a round table where Levi and Jace are sitting, their heads together as they talk. "I'm going to join my brothers."

"We're going to mingle," Lia says and takes my hand in hers. "Let's find Joy and Starla. I bet they're by the food."

"I could use food."

Sure enough, Joy and Starla are at the appetizer buffet, loading up tiny plates with canapes and crab cakes.

"I'm so happy you guys are here," Joy says with a sigh. "I mean, I've been coming to these things with Jace forever, but it's exhausting to try and make small talk when you don't know anyone, you know?"

"We've got you," Starla says. The pop star is

dressed in a killer strapless green dress that has a slit up the side to her hip. Red-soled heels are the perfect touch. She turns to me, a wide smile on her face. "Wow, girl, you clean up nice."

"It was all Amelia's doing. I can bake a cake like a champ, but I'm worthless when it comes to makeup."

"Good thing she has me," Amelia says with a wink.

While the other three chat about dresses and hairstyles, I glance around the room, not expecting to see anyone I know. I love my brother-in-law, but I don't walk in the same social circles as he does.

There's a glass sculpture in the middle of the room that I immediately recognize, and I wander away from the others to check it out.

Vivid red, orange, and yellow; twisty, swirling shapes that reach for the ceiling. I'd recognize the work anywhere.

This is an O'Callaghan piece.

I stand and sip my bubbly drink, examining the craftsmanship in the glass, then notice a discreet plaque that says it's part of the silent auction.

I'm positive that I can't afford it. His pieces go for thousands, sometimes *hundreds* of thousands of dollars.

My family is wealthy, but that's out of my price range.

But maybe, just maybe I can put in a bid.

I wander over to the silent auction bids and see

that the sculpture is already well into the six figures and kiss that dream goodbye.

Someday, maybe, I'll own one of Kane's pieces.

I shrug a shoulder and turn to walk away, almost colliding with a broad chest.

"Oh, pardon me," I say. When my eyes travel up the strong chest and over the recently shaven square jawline, I look into mossy green eyes.

Kane O'Callaghan.

"We meet again," he says with a small smile.

"It seems we do." I take a deep breath, and the smell of someone's perfume fills my nostrils. My lungs immediately tighten. As much as I want to stay and talk with him, ask him a million questions, I have to get to a restroom.

I need my rescue inhaler.

Damn it!

I take two big steps and begin the mental speech to talk me down from a full-on panic attack.

You're fine. You're breathing fine. Slow breaths, Anastasia. It's just a little perfume, that's all.

I try to smile his way, and then turn away again. I guess if I have a full-on asthma attack here and now, there are roughly forty-seven doctors who can save the day.

I walk into the women's restroom and open my clutch, pull out my inhaler, and take a long pull off it, relieved when the albuterol fills my lungs. I immediately feel relief.

See? You're fine. All better. No reason to panic.

Let's not even consider the fact that this is the second time in two days that I've managed to make a fool of myself in front of Kane.

I stuff the inhaler back into my clutch and walk out of the restroom where Kane is leaning against the wall, his hands in his pockets, looking casual and calm as he watches me walk through the door.

"Was it something I said?" he asks.

"I'm sorry, I didn't mean to rush off."

"All better?" His lips turn up in that half-smile.

"Better." I nod, not wanting to get into my medical issues. "That piece you donated is stunning."

"Thank you." He slips a hand out of his pocket and reaches out for mine. "Dance with me."

"*Dance* with you?"

He quirks an eyebrow. "Please."

WITH ME IN SEATTLE CHARACTER GLOSSARY

With more than twenty stories in the With Me In Seattle Series, I figured it was time to include a who's who in the world, listed by family. Please know this may contain spoilers for anyone who hasn't read all of the books, but it's a great reference for those who want to make sure they read about everyone.

The Williams Family

Luke Williams – Hollywood movie producer. Married to Natalie Williams, a professional photographer. Parents to Olivia, Keaton, Haley and Chelsea. {Come Away With Me}

Samantha Williams Nash – Professional. Married to mega rock star Leo Nash. {Rock With Me}

Mark Williams – Works in Construction, for Isaac Montgomery. Married to professional dancer Meredith

Summers. Parents to Lucy and Hudson. {Breathe With Me}

The Montgomery Family

Steven and Gail Montgomery – Parents of Isaac, Matt, Caleb, Will and Jules. Steven is the father of Dominic.

Isaac Montgomery – Eldest sibling. Owner for Montgomery Construction. Married to stay at home mom Stacy Montgomery. Parents to Sophie and Liam. {Under the Mistletoe With Me}

Matt Montgomery – Detective with the Seattle PD. Married to Nic Dalton Montgomery, the owner and baker at Succulent Sweets. Parents to Abigail and Finn. {Tied With Me}

Caleb Montgomery – Navy SEAL. Married to Brynna Vincent Montgomery. Parents to Josie, Maddie and Michael. {Safe With Me}

Will Montgomery – Quarterback for the Seattle professional football team. Married to Meg McBride Montgomery, a nurse at Seattle Children's Hospital. Parents to Erin and Zoey. {Play With Me}

Julianne (Jules) Montgomery McKenna – Entrepreneur. Married to Nate McKenna, the co-owner of their joint business. Parents to Stella. {Fight With Me}

Dominic Salvatore – Illegitimate son of Steven Montgomery. Owns vineyard and winery. Married to event planner Alecia. Parents to Emma. {Forever With Me}

Ed and Sherri Montgomery – Ed is Steven Montgomery's brother. Parents to Amelia, Anastasia and Archer.

Archer Montgomery – Eldest of the siblings. Real estate mogul. Married to Elena Watkins. {You Belong With Me}

Amelia Montgomery Crawford – YouTube sensation, makeup brand owner. Married to Wyatt Crawford, architect. {Stay With Me}

Anastasia Montgomery O'Callaghan – Wedding cake designer and baker. Married to Kane O'Callaghan, world-renown glass blowing artist. {Dream With Me}

The Crawford Family

Melody and Linus Crawford – Parents of Wyatt, Levi and Jace.

Wyatt Crawford – (Mentioned above) – {Stay With Me}

Jace Crawford – Best cardiothoracic surgeon on the west coast. Married to veterinarian Joy Thompson Crawford. {Love With Me}

Levi Crawford – Detective for Seattle PD. Married to mega pop star, Starla. {Dance With Me}

The O'Callaghan Family

Tom and Fiona O'Callaghan – Parents of Kane, Keegan, Shawn, Maeve and Maggie.

Kane O'Callaghan – referenced above. {Dream With Me}

Keegan O'Callaghan – Owner of O'Callaghan's Pub. Married to Isabella Harris. {Escape With Me}

Shawn O'Callaghan – Screenwriter. Married to Lexi Perry. {Imagine With Me}

Maeve O'Callaghan – Real Estate Agent. Married to Hunter Meyers. {Flirt With Me}

Margaret Mary O'Callaghan – Youngest sibling. Widowed. Married to Cameron Cox. {Take a Chance With Me}

The Martinelli and Watkins Family

Vinnie and Claudia Watkins – Deceased. Parents to Elena Watkins. Vinnie is the former boss of the mafia syndicate.

Carlo and Flavia Martinelli – Carlo is the current mob boss. Parents to Carmine, Shane and Rocco.

Elena Watkins – Referenced above. {You Belong With Me}

Carmine Martinelli – Eldest son. Mafioso. {Underboss}

Shane Martinelli – Middle son. Mafioso. {Headhunter}

Rocco Martinelli – Youngest son. Mafioso. {Off the Record}

Other Important People

Asher Smith – Former partner to Matt Montgomery. Now lives in New Orleans, married to Lila Bailey, a college professor. {Easy With You, a 1001 Dark Nights Novella}

Bailey Whitworth, Gray McDermitt, Kevin Welling – {Burn With Me}

Benjamin Demarco – Owner of Sound Fitness, a gym in downtown Seattle. {Shine With Me, a 1001 Dark Nights Novella}

Noel Thompson – Interior decorator. Sister to Joy Thompson. Married to Reed Taylor, a financial advisor. Parents to Piper. {Wonder With Me, a 1001 Dark Nights Novella}

NEWSLETTER SIGN UP

I hope you enjoyed reading this story as much as I enjoyed writing it! For upcoming book news, be sure to join my newsletter! I promise I will only send you news-filled mail, and none of the spam. You can sign up here:

https://mailchi.mp/kristenproby.com/newsletter-sign-up

ALSO BY KRISTEN PROBY:

Other Books by Kristen Proby

The With Me In Seattle Series

Come Away With Me - Luke & Natalie
Under The Mistletoe With Me - Isaac & Stacy
Fight With Me - Nate & Jules
Play With Me - Will & Meg
Rock With Me - Leo & Sam
Safe With Me - Caleb & Brynna
Tied With Me - Matt & Nic
Breathe With Me - Mark & Meredith
Forever With Me - Dominic & Alecia
Stay With Me - Wyatt & Amelia
Indulge With Me
Love With Me - Jace & Joy
Dance With Me Levi & Starla

ALSO BY KRISTEN PROBY:

You Belong With Me - Archer & Elena
Dream With Me - Kane & Anastasia
Imagine With Me - Shawn & Lexi
Escape With Me - Keegan & Isabella
Flirt With Me - Hunter & Maeve
Take a Chance With Me - Cameron & Maggie

Check out the full series here: https://www.kristenprobyauthor.com/with-me-in-seattle

Single in Seattle Series
The Secret - Vaughn & Olivia
The Scandal - Gray & Stella
The Score - Ike & Sophie

Check out the full series here: https://www.kristenprobyauthor.com/single-in-seattle

Huckleberry Bay Series

Lighthouse Way
Fernhill Lane
Chapel Bend

The Big Sky Universe

Love Under the Big Sky
Loving Cara

ALSO BY KRISTEN PROBY:

Seducing Lauren
Falling for Jillian
Saving Grace

The Big Sky
Charming Hannah
Kissing Jenna
Waiting for Willa
Soaring With Fallon

Big Sky Royal
Enchanting Sebastian
Enticing Liam
Taunting Callum

Heroes of Big Sky
Honor
Courage
Shelter

Check out the full Big Sky universe here: https://www.kristenprobyauthor.com/under-the-big-sky

Bayou Magic

Shadows
Spells
Serendipity

Check out the full series here: https://www.kristenprobyauthor.com/bayou-magic

The Curse of the Blood Moon Series

Hallows End
Cauldrons Call
Salems Song

The Romancing Manhattan Series

All the Way
All it Takes
After All

Check out the full series here: https://www.kristenprobyauthor.com/romancing-manhattan

The Boudreaux Series

Easy Love
Easy Charm
Easy Melody
Easy Kisses
Easy Magic
Easy Fortune
Easy Nights

Check out the full series here: https://www.kristenprobyauthor.com/boudreaux

The Fusion Series

Listen to Me
Close to You
Blush for Me
The Beauty of Us
Savor You

Check out the full series here: https://www.kristenprobyauthor.com/fusion

From 1001 Dark Nights

Easy With You
Easy For Keeps
No Reservations
Tempting Brooke
Wonder With Me
Shine With Me
Change With Me
The Scramble
Cherry Lane

Kristen Proby's Crossover Collection

ALSO BY KRISTEN PROBY:

Soaring with Fallon, A Big Sky Novel

Wicked Force: A Wicked Horse Vegas/Big Sky Novella
By Sawyer Bennett

All Stars Fall: A Seaside Pictures/Big Sky Novella
By Rachel Van Dyken

Hold On: A Play On/Big Sky Novella
By Samantha Young

Worth Fighting For: A Warrior Fight Club/Big Sky Novella
By Laura Kaye

Crazy Imperfect Love: A Dirty Dicks/Big Sky Novella
By K.L. Grayson

Nothing Without You: A Forever Yours/Big Sky Novella
By Monica Murphy

Check out the entire Crossover Collection here:
https://www.kristenprobyauthor.com/kristen-proby-crossover-collection

ABOUT THE AUTHOR

Kristen Proby has published more than sixty titles, many of which have hit the USA Today, New York Times and Wall Street Journal Bestsellers lists.

Kristen and her husband, John, make their home in her hometown of Whitefish, Montana with their two cats and dog.

- facebook.com/booksbykristenproby
- instagram.com/kristenproby
- bookbub.com/profile/kristen-proby
- goodreads.com/kristenproby

Printed in Great Britain
by Amazon